"I'm not here for your entertainment, Rader," Fancy whispered.

"I didn't ask you to be."

"Then why did you invite me here for the summer?" If Fancy kept asking, maybe one day she'd get the right answer.

"Curiosity."

"Yours or mine?" she asked.

"For right now, Fancy, mine."

When Rader's head bent toward her, she waited with anticipation, her eyes drifting shut as his lips brushed hers. When his mouth closed over hers, all thought fled. She felt only his lips. She clung to him, moving into his arms without full comprehension of what was happening.

It was a dream. A dream she'd cherished for years. And its reality was as sweet as she had hoped....

Dear Reader,

Welcome to Silhouette Romance—experience the magic of the wonderful world where two people fall in love. Meet heroines who will make you cheer for their happiness, and heroes (be they the boy next door or a handsome, mysterious stranger) who will win your heart. Silhouette Romance reflects the magic of love—sweeping you away with books that will make you laugh and cry; heartwarming, poignant stories that will move you time and time again.

In the next few months, we're publishing romances by many of your all-time favorites such as Diana Palmer, Brittany Young, Annette Broadrick and many others. Your response to these authors and others in Silhouette Romance has served as a touchstone for us, and we're pleased to bring you more books with Silhouette's distinctive medley of charm, wit and—above all—*romance*.

During 1991, we have many special events planned. Don't miss our WRITTEN IN THE STARS series. Each month in 1991, we're proud to present you with a book that focuses on the hero—and his astrological sign.

I hope you'll enjoy this book and all of the stories to come. Come home to romance—Silhouette Romance—for always!

Sincerely,

Tara Gavin
Senior Editor

OLIVIA FERRELL

Summer Fancy

Published by Silhouette Books New York

America's Publisher of Contemporary Romance

SILHOUETTE BOOKS
300 E. 42nd St., New York, N.Y. 10017

SUMMER FANCY

ISBN: 0-373-08768-3

First Silhouette Books printing January 1991

Printed in the U.S.A.

Books by Olivia Ferrell

Silhouette Special Edition

Love Has Its Reasons #48

Silhouette Romance

Crystal Angel #330
Cajun Man #467
High Rider #505
Summer Fancy #768

OLIVIA FERRELL

was born and raised in Missouri. Having worked in various fields from modeling to advertising to radio broadcasting, she tried her hand at writing in 1981. When not reading or writing romances, Olivia divides her time between her three children and her husband, Tom, who is a successful artist.

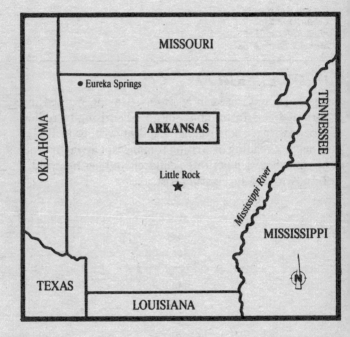

Chapter One

The bus from San Francisco whooshed to a stop, releasing its air brakes to echo in the late afternoon stillness of the small Arkansas town. From her seat near the back of the bus, Fancy Connors studied the small group of people awaiting its arrival. With a keen sense of apprehension, she saw Rader waiting for her.

Fancy had known Rader Malone as a stepbrother during the stormy marriage of her mother and his father. Fancy had been a preteen in this same rural area, living in the house that was now Rader's. The prospect of returning to the house where they'd all lived together during a tumultuous time in her life brought a flood of conflicting feelings and memories.

Rader had been her hero then, floating in and out of her life like something not quite real. She'd loved him with all the passion of a young girl of thirteen teetering between childhood and adulthood. He'd considered her a bothersome temporary sibling—temporary because the marriage between their parents was doomed from the beginning.

It was because of the strain of that marriage upon all involved that Fancy knew Rader probably wished he hadn't obeyed the impulse to invite her to spend the summer at the remote ranch he'd inherited from his father. He was probably wishing she hadn't snapped at the chance to come.

Rader couldn't know that coming "home" was an act of desperation on her part. His house was the only place she'd ever felt at home. The others had only been temporary places. Added to that was a desperation born of knowing she had to find out once and for all whether what she felt for Rader was love or the residual of childhood infatuation.

Now Fancy was afraid she'd made an awful mistake. Maybe the dream was better than the reality. But she'd made the decision to get on with her life. Settling her feelings for Rader Malone was the first step.

Fancy drew a deep breath to steady her nerves as she studied the man waiting for her. Trying to read Rader's attitude by his stance, Fancy catalogued the differences between the man he was now and the boy he had been.

Rader was tall and ruggedly handsome. He drew second glances from the occasional passing female. The early summer weather necessitated a light jacket, but where most of the male population opted for jeans and windbreakers, Rader was casually dressed in slacks and a matching jacket of tobacco brown. A cream-colored oxford shirt made his swarthy skin appear even darker. She couldn't tell much more because he remained in the shadow of the bus station porch.

Rader had watched the bus draw to a stop. Straightening from his lounging position he stood, legs spread, arms folded, to await his guest. He was tired. He'd been tired at the funeral—probably the reason he'd made the mistake of asking her to stay at the ranch this summer. She'd been so pale, so shaken by having to face the reality of her mother's death in such a terrible way, that he'd given in.

Rader shook his head. What had he been thinking, to invite her here? Fancy had a streak of independence a mile wide, which was, he knew, the result of having such a careless mother. Fancy was a survivor, much like her mother. But then, there were a number of similarities between Fancy and the selfish woman who was a mother in name only. Knowing her independence and that Fancy was well aware of how he felt about Mona, why had she accepted the invitation?

He had mixed feelings about her visit. Fancy had been in the back of his mind for years, like the wisp of a dream. Though he'd told himself a thousand times she wasn't right for him, that she was too much like Mona, Fancy had remained with him in memory. Her charm, her smile, her strangely golden wise-owl eyes had clung to him like the silken strands of a spider's web.

Perhaps it was curiosity, along with a desire to validate his attitudes toward her, that had made him ask Fancy to come. In spite of everything logical he told himself about Fancy—and about Mona—he could never get her out of his mind. He'd never married, and he was very much afraid that Fancy might just be the reason he had not.

Even as a youngster, there had been something about her that was totally captivating. Fancy wove a spell around everyone she met, and he'd been caught in her magic. Even later, when he had proof Mona had stamped Fancy in her image, she still played in his memory like a melody he couldn't forget.

His mind reversed to a couple of years earlier. The last time he'd seen Fancy. It had been in a bar in San Francisco. His being there had been by happenstance. His trip to San Francisco had been business. He'd just closed a deal for a movie to be made from his second novel and as a gesture of good manners, he'd agreed to toast the venture with a late-night drink. His associate had suggested they stop in at The Blue Note, a small intimate bar that was growing in popularity, and check out the new entertainment.

Rader had agreed reluctantly. He'd wanted to return to his hotel and go to bed. The west-coast trip had taken longer than planned, and he'd been ready to go to the farm in the Arkansas hills he'd grown to love. But they'd gone in, been seated at a corner table and ordered. When Fancy stepped into the spotlight, he had almost choked on his drink.

Even after several years, Rader had recognized her immediately. That wise-owl look was well remembered. But when she stood at the microphone and sang a sexy blues number, he could hardly believe what he was seeing and hearing.

Even now, his stomach knotted when he remembered the shimmering figure swathed in a midnight-blue sequined sheath dress, her shoulders bare and glowing in the spotlight. Her hair had been left hanging free, shining like a pale curtain down her back. Her voice had been low and husky and strong, plucking at the heart, tearing at his insides.

He'd glanced around the crowded room and realized every man there felt as he did. She was earthy, untouchable. A flame that drew with its danger. She was tangible and she was not; she was the vision of everything a woman was and what every man wanted his woman to be. He'd felt it and recognized it as an echo of the woman his father had married—the woman who had speeded the end of the man's life. Rader had choked down instant desire. Fancy had never known he was there.

He'd left The Blue Note that night with disappointment and a tinge of bitterness coloring the fond memories he'd held of a young Francine. He'd wanted to believe she'd not succumbed to Mona's influence, but seeing her there in that bar, singing to the men, appealing to each one individually, had shattered the last shred of illusion that Fancy was still the naive little girl he'd known. It had left an emptiness in him he still couldn't fill.

That had been almost three years ago. He'd not seen her and had tried not to think about her since. Until the funeral.

Rader gritted his teeth unconsciously again. Like mother, like daughter; blood will tell. He called up all the worn clichés he could think of to dull the keen edge of desire cutting into him as he watched the last passenger step down from the bus. He couldn't allow himself to be twisted around her little finger as he was sure she would try to do.

If Fancy was anything like Mona, she was here for money, for security, a larger piece of the estate pie and a chance at the fine things his success could buy her. She had agreed to return to this little "backwater" place, away from the glitter of the big city, because it meant someone to take care of her and buy her pretty things. Of course, he did go to New York and Los Angeles on business quite frequently. Perhaps often enough to satisfy her, for a while, as his father had tried to satisfy Mona.

Fancy was framed by the doorway. She stood as if she owned the world, then swung to the ground with lithe grace. His gaze swept over her. Reluctantly, he acknowledged that even without makeup and special lighting, she was a beautiful woman. But so had her mother been.

Rader studied Fancy's rather rumpled appearance, comparing it with the last time he'd seen her. Tawny hair, drawn to the side behind one ear and bound with a band, fell to her waist. The simplicity of the style left the classic lines of her face free, revealing slightly slanted pale golden eyes slumberously alert beneath gently curving eyebrows.

He sucked in his breath. She was beautiful. Every bit as beautiful and naturally sensual as her mother had been. But there were differences. Subtle ones, but differences nonetheless. Or was he only deluding himself?

Mona had been flashy with a brittle edge. Fancy was softer, with a quietly waiting beauty that sneaked up on a man and captured him. Her face was a photographer's dream. A straight nose balanced high prominent cheekbones. Her chin was rounded and determined. Alone, her face would have presented a provocative picture. But the skin-tight jeans, stretching over too-thin hip bones and encasing incredibly long, narrow legs to fall in tattered hems above scuffed boots, evidenced the bohemian life-style he expected she lived.

She took the last step, and Rader's breath caught in his throat. The thin T-shirt she wore was stretched over surprisingly full breasts and boasted Rod's Speed Shop from point to point, with the stencil of a motorcycle just below. A down vest, hanging open, was her only jacket. Long hands with equally long fingers clutched a red duffel bag that had seen better days.

Fancy stood a step away from the bus's door, the bag slung over her shoulder. A hip-slung stance fairly shouted arrogance. Rader sensed she wasn't about to make the first move.

Fancy watched him, waiting, measuring him. She recognized the maturity he'd gained since they were briefly of one family. He was heavier, his body more compact. She fought revealing the nervousness that made her stomach roll, and sought to exhibit more confidence than she could ever muster.

They'd had no opportunity to talk at any length at the funeral, and she'd had only an impression of the changes in him. But seeing him now, she realized

Rader was every bit as good-looking as she'd remembered. And he stirred her just as deeply.

Finally the dual appraisal ended. Rader strode forward in that easy, gliding style of a man completely at ease with his body. He was the same as she remembered in that way. He was older, matured, more handsome and apparently as enigmatic as ever—and just as wary of her, if the distant look in his eyes meant anything. The sight of him taunted her senses, but he looked as if he could easily reconsider his offer of a long visit at the farm.

Fancy squared her shoulders. Well, she was here for the summer. Three months. There was nowhere else for her to go, so she might as well see this through.

As Rader approached, Fancy found her gaze drawn to his hair. It was as full and as black as she remembered. When he was younger, he'd refused to have it cut even though Kurt, his father, had threatened to shave his head. A Stetson hat had shaded his dark eyes earlier, but they were as penetrating as ever as he studied her in return, the hat in his right hand, tapping impatiently against his thigh.

He'd changed some. The hint of maleness at twenty had deepened. His dark-eyed gaze held experience and laconic laziness with sensual overtones inherent to his nature. He made her fully aware that she was a woman.

"Hello...Fancy." His baritone voice was low, controlled, giving only a hint of irritation as he hesitated over the name she now used.

"Rader."

"Have a good trip?"

"Yes. Thanks again for inviting me to your home," Fancy said, controlling the breathiness of excitement that threatened her self-assured facade.

"It was your home, too."

"Was," she emphasized.

His gaze swept over her again in deliberation. Her face tightened, and her finely carved, full-lipped mouth firmed in determination. He wasn't going to make this easy.

"That's all your luggage?" His gaze touched the duffel bag.

"That's right."

"Then let's go." He picked up her duffel and strode away, leaving her to follow. Fancy did, her gaze boring into his long, wide-shouldered back. Releasing a long, silent sigh, Fancy renewed her determination to see this through if it killed her. She'd vowed to find out if what she felt for Rader was real or a dream, but she almost wished she'd kept the dream.

Fancy hoped it wouldn't take long to get to the house. She was bone tired. The bus ride had been long and stuffy. Unventilated cigarette smoke had made her stomach queasy, and since she hadn't eaten anything all day, her head ached.

Rader flicked a hand toward a black Bronco, which had one decorative stripe down its side, indicating she should get in on the passenger side. Fancy pulled open the door and stepped up into the high-based vehicle, wincing a little at the twinge of pain in her stomach. She should have eaten something. The doctor had warned her that while her anemia was corrected, her ulcer wasn't. She needed to pay special attention to eating properly. Plus, she hadn't taken her medication all day. Now she was paying for it. She'd had no idea an ulcer could be so debilitating.

Fancy folded into the bucket seat, briefly resting her head against the back. What a mess her life had become. Just when she had been convincing herself she had everything in control, it had all fallen apart emotionally and physically. Rader's offer gave her time to recover and decide what to do next.

Rader slid his lean frame in beside her and scooted down into the seat comfortably, then started the engine.

"I wasn't sure you'd come." He stared out the windshield, his hands resting on the steering wheel as the Bronco idled.

"Sorry you asked me?" Fancy held her breath.

He turned his dark gaze upon her, doubt obvious in the set of his features. "Perhaps you'll be sorry you came. I'm afraid there's not much to do here."

His terse comment made her defensive. "I'm not here to be entertained. Just to relax. To...spend some time on the farm. It's been a long time...."

"Is that all?"

But before she could say anything more, he put the Bronco in gear and gunned the engine as he drove away from the curb. I've made a fool of myself, she thought, staring out the window. A complete and utter fool. Ten years was a long time to cling to a silly dream.

The passing scene of the small town was, she knew, typical of southwest Missouri and northern Arkansas. Fancy studied it with curiosity. Not much had changed. It was the last place she would have pictured for Rader Malone to choose for his home. But, she supposed, his ties here were very strong.

The one main street boasted a general store, dry goods, mart, a combination drug and dime store, a feed store, a small café. On side streets, small frame houses rested, their lawns neatly trimmed and fenced. It was late enough in the afternoon that families were just sitting down to dinner, and the streets were virtually empty. Only a lone pick-up truck passed them as they headed out into the countryside.

"I was sorry I couldn't stay after the funeral," Rader said, "or able to help you with anything."

"I thought perhaps you didn't want to."

"I admit, I had my doubts about going at all. I didn't want to be a hypocrite. But I wanted to be sure you didn't need anything."

"You were never a hypocrite, Rader. You were always brutally honest in your feelings about Mona."

"Mona was an exciting and stimulating, but shallow woman. My father, unfortunately, was enchanted by her."

"And mother might had even loved him a little."

Rader darted a glance at her. "You sound a little doubtful. You were always her champion before."

"Nothing's changed. She was my mother, and I loved her, but even I had to face reality after a while." The truth had hurt. Hurt a lot.

"What do you mean?" He sounded wary, and she thought he had a right to be.

"Mona wasn't the faithful kind, Rader. You know that. And Kurt was a workaholic. The nights were late and Mona needed entertainment.'' She tossed off the words, holding the pain close inside.

"Just what are you saying?" In spite of himself, Rader wanted the answers to questions that had lain dormant in his mind for years.

"Nothing. Mona was...Mona." Fancy drew a deep breath. "I'm sorry. I shouldn't...it does no good to speak badly of her."

"You're right. Memories should be pleasant," was Rader's only comment.

Yes, Fancy said to herself. But can you know how seeing you again stirs up bittersweet memories, memories of subtle psychological warfare waged in that opulent household we shared, mixed with the times I cried on your shoulder and you told me everything would be all right? But they weren't, were they? Nothing was ever made right.

Fancy rested her head against the seat, allowing it to roll to one side as she watched darkness come over the landscape. The house was set deep in the Ozark Hills, in an area steeped with history and an aura of mystery. As a child, she'd fantasized about the famous outlaws who had drifted through the area in the late 1800s, and the more infamous who had used the isolated pockets of forest and mountain as hiding places.

"I'd forgotten how far out in the boonies the farm is."

He glanced at her profile again. She was pale, and dark smudges of weariness shadowed her eyes. Obviously the life she led was beginning to exact its price early. She was, after all, only twenty-four. In spite of himself, Rader wanted to see to it that she rested away those shadows while she was here.

"It's not much farther. The turnoff is just up ahead." He slowed and turned off the highway onto a blacktop road. "It's a real working farm now. We raise horses, some crops, some cattle."

"I can't imagine you a farmer."

Rader said nothing, stung a little by her dry comment.

By this time, the open landscape had turned to great gray bluffs of limestone covered with lichen and moss. Small cedars clung tenaciously to crevices and to nearly bald hilltops while great oaks populated the forest edge around the valley. The whole effect in the growing darkness before moonlight lit the countryside was one of an eeriness and mystique that spoke to her quiet inner self.

Rader slowed the Bronco and turned onto a lane that was only slightly wider than the vehicle. Fancy sat up in the seat to get a glimpse of the house.

"Did Brian see you to the bus?"

Fancy glanced at him, remembering the resentment she'd felt at his sending a stranger to help her with arrangements. Brian Carter was Rader's attorney and he'd helped with the funeral and more.

"You know he did. He was very efficient. Just as you knew he'd be."

Rader caught back a sharp retort. After all, he'd known she'd resent him sending a stranger in his place. In some sense, he guessed, he'd sent Brian to make sure Fancy would be all right and to make sure she came today, without involving himself.

He drew a deep breath. He didn't know why he'd invited her, really, but he had to know...what? That she was like Mona? Or that she was less tantalizing than he remembered? In any event, the end result would be to quiet old ghosts.

"Brian doesn't deserve your criticism. I was in New York completing some business I couldn't postpone when word came of Mona's death. He was kind enough to fill in for me. By the time I could get free, everything was done except the funeral. In fact, I'm just on my way back or I would have had you come in at another town."

"Thanks."

Irritation marked his handsome face. "Fancy, there was no love lost between me and Mona. But I wouldn't have wished her dead. Nor did I like the idea of you facing everything alone. I did the best I could at the time."

Fancy swallowed the hint of tears that threatened. "I know. I'm sorry. I'm...just a little tired," she excused herself. But it was the memories that brought the tears.

Mona. Momma...yet Fancy had never been able to call her mother that. She was dead, her lovely provocative body smashed in a private plane crash along with that of her most recent conquest.

As if reading her mind, Rader spoke again. "Who was the man Mona was with?"

"A Texas oilman."

"Where had they been?" Rader ignored the edginess in Fancy's voice.

"In Texas, where else? Some charity ball that 'simply couldn't be missed,'" Fancy quoted.

"How long had she been gone?"

Fancy frowned. Why was he asking these questions? What difference did it make to him where Mona had been, who she was with or how long she'd been gone? "A week, ten days, two weeks. I don't remember exactly when she left."

"Did she leave for long periods frequently?"

Fancy shrugged. "Mona did what Mona wanted to do."

"You're not answering my question."

"Look, let's just drop the subject of my mother." She wished he'd just forget Mona and concentrate on her and the present. Not the past.

But typically, Rader was persistent. "Why don't you want to answer my questions, Fancy? Weren't you home when Mona left?" Something he might call jealousy, but didn't want to, sat like a stone in his stomach. "Who were you living with?"

Anger and weariness prompted her sharp retort. "Where I was is none of your business. Besides, it isn't important."

"If it's so unimportant, why won't you just answer my questions?"

Fancy's hand clenched into a fist on her thigh. Rader had always been stubborn, but she could be, too. Sympathy had prompted his invitation, and she'd taken advantage of it, but she wouldn't again. She was here to learn something about herself and about Rader. If he felt sorry for her, sorry that she'd been sick, sorry she didn't have any money and couldn't pay her bills, then she wouldn't be able to tell how he honestly felt about her.

She stared out the window. It was full dark outside now. Not a light broke the inky blackness. What a strange sight, Fancy thought. She didn't remember it being so dark. San Francisco was never dark. There were always lights, action, people.

"Answer me... Fancy. Did Mona often leave for extended periods of time?"

Demanding patience of her frayed nerves, Fancy drew a resigned breath. "As I said, Rader, it's been a long time since she lived with your father. And it's been a long time since I was young enough to need supervision."

"I always thought it was strange neither of them ever filed for divorce."

"Mona did," Fancy said, "but Kurt never signed the papers. At least, that's what she told me. They just never picked it up again."

Fancy continued to stare out at the darkness. Rader had to believe she was here just for a vacation. She needed time for him to get to know her as herself, not as Mona's daughter. It might be too late, but she had to try. She had to know if there was any hope for them together.

Her reluctance to answer his questions made Rader even more curious. He was determined to know exactly what had happened... to Mona and to Fancy.

"Is that how it was then? They couldn't live together, but couldn't end it, either. Then, ever since Kurt died, Mona floated around the country living on the, shall we say, gratuities of her men friends?"

Fancy shifted to a more comfortable position in the seat, crossing one leg over the other, resting one slim hand on her knee. "That's a very succinct way of putting it, Rader. I can see why you're such a successful novelist. What were you doing in New York? Signing an agreement for yet another movie based on yet another bestselling book? 'R. C. Malone has the Midas touch.' Isn't that what I read in some tabloid or other not long ago? Six novels in six years with three already made into critically acclaimed and financially successful motion pictures. Quite a record, Rader."

But Rader wasn't distracted. "You're very adroitly evading the issue. What did you do while Mona was away? Did you have a job, go to college, live with someone?" It was the last question that nagged at him persistently.

Fancy cursed his singlemindedness. "No, Rader, I didn't go to college. I'm not the honors material you were. Must have something to do with the genes," she said, trying to swallow the hurt. "But, I do have my talents."

"Undoubtedly," he commented. She hadn't answered the question about living with someone, and it irritated him.

Rader's face was grim as he carefully guided the Bronco along the narrow road. They maneuvered a curve and approached the large two-story house that, in her mind, had retained all the markings of a castle.

Created of native limestone, the structure blended into the hillside that stood at its back. It squatted there solidly, arrogantly, as if it had stood for centuries and would stand for many more. For Fancy it had always represented a stability that otherwise had been missing in her life.

Rader brought the Bronco to a halt at steps leading up across the terraced lawn. In the weak early moonlight, the house took on a waiting, almost Gothic quality.

Fancy remembered sitting on the front porch in the spring, daydreaming, sometimes waiting for Rader to come home. She'd walked in the woods, wishing he was there beside her. "You live here alone?"

"Would it bother you if I didn't?" Perverseness prompted his response.

"You have to admit it's quite a departure from a San Francisco apartment," she said. She must be careful. If she prodded him too much, he could easily turn around and put her back on the bus.

Rader drew a deep breath. No sense in creating more hostility between them. She might decide not to stay and...well, he didn't want her leaving just yet. He wouldn't examine his reasons right now. They might not bear too much scrutiny.

"Mrs. Sartin comes in mornings now to clean and prepare meals. You remember her?"

Fancy's hands clenched together in nervousness, but she kept her voice level. "Yes. She had two children, didn't she? A boy and girl?"

"Umm-hum. They both still live at home."

Well, not a lot had changed here. But that was good. She wanted time and opportunity to learn more about Rader. Now she had it.

Sliding slowly from the Bronco, Fancy slung the duffel bag to her shoulder with practiced ease. She followed Rader up the stone walk to the front door of the larger-than-life house, watching him stride along in his loose-limbed way. The place was so familiar yet so different, and Rader was so changed that she was entirely intimidated.

Maybe she had made a mistake. Maybe she should have just left her dreams alone and gone on with her life. Maybe, but she wasn't entirely convinced just yet.

Chapter Two

The house had always looked old, solid, as if it had been born out of the rocks of the ground upon which it sat. The front door was fitted with wrought-iron hinges and handle. It swung open easily, and Fancy followed Rader through, stopping just inside to absorb the unexpected decor.

It had been a showplace when she and Mona had lived there, but now it was quietly elegant.

The entry floor was polished wood. A large woven rug in a geometric design of earthen-tone squares set at angles rested in the middle of the wide entrance. There was an aroma of sandalwood. The sound of silence.

Fancy dropped her duffel bag onto the floor as she continued to study her surroundings, the soft thud loud in the silence of the house. She studied what she could see of the interior, measuring it against what she remembered. Everything was different. Improvements that helped keep the memories from being overwhelming.

"Well, what do you think?" He'd watched her appraisal with interest.

Fancy had almost forgotten Rader was waiting. "I like it. I like the Shaker-like simplicity of the living room, the American primitive. Where did you find the French shipping jug?"

A lifted eyebrow indicated his surprise at her knowledge. "On a trip to Haiti about a year ago. How did you know what it was?"

She shrugged a delicate shoulder. "I didn't live with Mona for nothing. She may have been a frivolous person, but she knew the value of things. Antique as well as contemporary."

"I see," was all he could say. "Well, let me show you your room, then how about something to eat?"

"Fine." Her stomach hurt so badly now that she wanted to bend over. But she walked carefully, with shoulders back, so Rader wouldn't know. Once she was settled in her room, maybe she could take her medication.

The bedroom to which Rader led her had been hers, but it was so different now. The bed sitting between wide windows in the pink-and-peach room was an eighteenth-century butterfly, complete with lined bedcurtains. Fancy was overwhelmed.

Plush carpeting taunted her tired feet, her toes wanting to bury themselves in the soft, pink floor covering. Pale watercolors of misty mornings and flowers graced the walls. A lounge chair, also in pale

pink, with darker pink throw pillows scattered care-
lessly across it, sat in front of a window. A maple sec-
retary with a fragile chair was opposite.

"Well, you successfully wiped out all traces of our
living here," she said. Rader had always made hateful remarks about Mona's taste in decorating. The
house had evidenced the Malone wealth but nothing
like this.

Rader's stance was loose-limbed, but there was la-
tent power in his seemingly relaxed body and inten-
sity in his dark gaze. "You never let up, do you,
Fancy?" A lazy, indulgent smile softened the chastis-
ing quality of the statement.

Her breath caught and their gazes held, each si-
lently questioning the other. Fancy wondered if the
summer would be full of their tearing at each other.

Rader took that moment to further assess the
changes in her. She was more beautiful than ever, but
there was an air of fragility about her that appealed to
his inherent need to protect. There was something
about her that fairly shouted vulnerability in spite of
her prickly defensiveness.

He sensed that the defensiveness was a protective
shield and he wondered why she felt it was necessary.
Subconsciously, Rader knew that if they got to the
point of letting down defenses with each other, they
would be opening up a whole other list of problems.

It's going to be one hell of a long summer, but an
interesting one, he told himself. Definitely interesting.

"Come down when you've freshened up. I'll put
together something for us to eat."

He left her standing in the middle of the room, feeling dejected, tired and very alone. Maybe it was a mistake coming, but it was too late to back out now.

Fancy went into the bathroom and found it matched the bedroom with its pink-and-white floor tile and wallpaper. She wished she had time to run a tub full of hot water and soak for a very long time.

Instead, she rummaged in her bag for a brush and ran it through her hair. Its length waved out to form wings on either side of her face, so to control it she fashioned a thick plait that fell to the center of her back. She fastened it with a white ribbon she found in the bottom of the duffel bag.

Spilling two pills from a bottle into her palm, she swallowed them with a sip of water, then splashed her face and patted it dry. "Okay, back into the fray," she murmured to herself.

Fancy stepped out into the hall. One bedroom was between hers and the stairs. As she passed it, curiosity prompted her to peek inside.

The room had been Kurt's, but obviously it now belonged to Rader. She stepped inside. The colonial decor of the living room was here in the bedspread, which was a copy of an 1860 mariner's-compass quilt in browns, oranges and greens. The carpeting was a continuation of the brown plush shag of the hallway. The bed was a cannonball that Fancy judged to be at least king-size, but she forced her gaze away from it. It conjured up too many dreams, stirred too many desires.

Allowing her gaze to sweep the thoroughly masculine room, she stepped to the double-doored closet.

The doors were slightly ajar and the sleeve of a tweed sports coat was caught between them.

Fancy touched it, her fingertips sensitive to the soft fabric. Pulling the door open, she gazed at the clothes hanging there. Obeying an impulse, she brushed her cheek with the coat sleeve and caught the lingering aroma of his cologne. She closed her eyes and breathed deeply of his identity. Oh, Rader. Is it too late? Was it always too late?

Realizing she'd spent too much time exploring, Fancy strode quickly out of the room. Following her nose to the kitchen, she pushed open the door to find a room that was the epitome of modern excellence.

Rader was busy at the stove but looked up when she entered. "How does an omelette with ham, mushrooms and cheese sound?"

"Delicious," Fancy said, sliding onto a stool at the bar where she could watch Rader slide a perfect omelette onto a plate beside slices of toast.

"Eat," he said, a smile softening the command.

The omelette was even better than it smelled—light, fluffy, perfectly turned and marvelously seasoned with herbs and spices Fancy couldn't name. She ate ravenously, ignoring Rader, who sat on a stool beside her. She began to feel better immediately. Rader poured them each a cup of steaming coffee.

They didn't talk while they ate. It wasn't until the last scrap of egg was gone and Fancy had poured a second coffee for each of them that Rader lounged against the bar and swept his measuring gaze over her long-limbed beauty.

"You've grown up, Fancy. That gawky thirteen-year-old I first met had freckles, I remember, and that same taffy hair in a pony tail. You were all legs and arms and teeth. When you grinned, you grinned all over."

She cut an aggrieved look in his direction. "I hoped you'd forget that. You weren't around much and you were much too old to bother with a gawky thirteen-year-old."

A small smile curved his lips. "You have to remember I was rather impressed with my collegiate status. The only time I was free was semester break and, if I remember, you traveled a lot with Mona and Dad, when he was free. There just wasn't time."

"No, there wasn't much time."

"We had our good times, when you weren't being a pest." His dark eyes glinted with humor.

She remembered only a few times that he'd exhibited humor. Of course, many things had changed. He had changed. Physically as well as psychologically.

Where there had been a brooding quality about him, now there was blatant sensuality. At thirteen and fourteen she hadn't realized so fully the potency of his maleness. Then it had been something dreams were made of. Now she could put a name to it, but her mind skittered away from doing so. It made what she felt far too real, too potent, far too soon.

Physically, Rader had hardened, had come into his own. His features were strong, the jaw determined, his chin holding just the hint of a cleft, his mouth generous. His eyebrows were slanted, a frown line just forming between them as if he frowned unconsciously in concentration. Some things hadn't changed. Though in a different way, he was just as intriguing as he'd ever been.

For months after their first meeting, she'd struggled with infatuation, his dark eyes haunting her dreams. His eyes were dark brown, defying a definite color description. She remembered, though, that they turned a stormy black when he was angry, a warm chocolate when he laughed.

Rader did have a temper. She'd seen its quickness firsthand when Mona's demands exceeded Rader's ability to humor her. She remembered, too, that when Rader set his mind on something, he was rarely deterred. It was this stubborn streak that had brought about the break between Rader and his father. Neither of them would swallow pride and make the first move to bring them back together. Their differences over Mona had been the biggest obstacle.

Breaking the silence that Rader had allowed to stretch, Fancy slid from the stool and carried her plate to the sink. When she turned around, Rader was studying her intently. Suddenly nervous, she ran damp palms down her jean-clad thighs. From the look in those dark, unfathomable eyes, Fancy knew her respite from questioning was at an end. She was surprised at his query.

"What did Brian Carter tell you?"

Fancy struggled to keep her calm facade in place. Hitching herself carefully up on the end of the cabinet, she sat hunched over, elbows resting on knees. In this position, she was slightly above Rader, which made her feel a bit more in control of the situation.

She studied the toes of her scuffed boots. "Not a lot. Just that he was, is, your attorney. He arrived the day after the crash, just in time to handle all the arrangements. He took care of everything. It . . . made things much easier for me. Thanks for sending him."

Brian Carter was a lot like Rader. He'd practically railroaded her into decisions, including the one to close the apartment and have Mona's things stored for a while. She wasn't even certain where he'd arranged storage.

"I didn't want you to have to handle things alone. Mona's death, especially in that way, must have been quite a shock. From what Brian said, you weren't handling the situation very well."

"How did you feel . . ." She shrugged away the rest of the question. She knew how Rader felt about Mona.

"It doesn't matter how I felt about her. She was your mother."

Fancy met his dark gaze evenly. "Our . . . relationship wasn't perhaps what you might expect. I was the unhappy reminder of a brief affair with a very talented but unsuccessful musician. An affair that lasted only six months or so, I was told, before he found someone else to bankroll his struggling career."

"It always bothered you that . . . Mona and your father weren't married."

She glanced at him. "You knew?"

"I have for a long time."

"I see." Breaking eye contact, she forced her hands to relax and leaned back on her elbows to stare at the ceiling. A nagging ache was growing behind her eyes, but she wouldn't give in to it. She couldn't afford to display any sign of weakness in front of Rader. She had to deal with him on even ground.

"Mona told me herself."

His eyes darkened as he studied her. His hands rested on the woodgrain bar top as he leaned forward on his forearms. His long body shifted easily, the contours of his muscled shoulders and biceps rippling beneath the close-fitting shirt.

"I...think I'll go upstairs," Fancy said, just wanting to go somewhere and hide. She slid easily off the cabinet and didn't miss the speculative look in Rader's eyes as his gaze encountered the skimpy T-shirt stretched over her generous, unfettered breasts.

A faint blush touched her cheeks as she turned away, unwilling to see the accusing look that would be in his eyes. After all, she was Mona's daughter. Suddenly it seemed hopeless to think she might be able to change the image he held of her as a second Mona Connors. Despair and weariness swept over her in a wave.

"I'll go to bed now, Rader. It was a long trip...."

Rader slid to his feet, hooking his thumbs into the belt of his slacks while spearing her with a look of fierce determination. "Mona was your mother. Why don't you like talking about her?"

"She's gone. It's no use raking over old coals. You, of all people, should want to let her go."

When she moved toward the door again, Rader reached out and caught her braid. "I'll get my answers, Fancy. I always do." When she didn't respond, he continued. "You might as well tell me why you're here."

She thought about it. For just a moment. Then all this tension would be over. But she'd come with a purpose. A purpose that would determine the direction of her future. They needed time to get to know each other as people. It was too early to surrender.

"There's nothing, Rader. Nothing."

His husky voice strummed her taut nerves. "'O what a tangled web we weave, when first we practice to deceive...!'" The words were almost whispered.

She'd thought she could handle being with Rader, but she'd been wrong. The tangled strands of her own web of deceit were pulling tight around her, and walking away wouldn't be easy if this thing between herself and Rader had only the substance of desire and not love.

Fancy tried to step away, but he held on to her hair. Her golden eyes narrowed at his refusal to release her.

"What . . ." she began.

"Fancy. How did you come by that name? When I knew you, it was Francine."

Shrugging her shoulders, Fancy looked away from his questioning gaze. "It started as a joke and just stuck. You know how those things are."

When she looked back at him, Fancy's apprehension grew. The speculative look had returned to his shadowed eyes.

"I don't know the real reason you're here, but I'm intrigued by your reluctance to talk to me. When something interests me, I investigate. And I find answers, Fancy. Just remember that."

Fancy finally pulled her hair free but when she stepped away again, he caught her wrist. Her breath caught as he turned her hand palm up.

"I noticed these callouses while we were eating. What caused them?"

Fancy returned his questioning gaze levelly but sought refuge from his probing questions in a flip response. "Why, polishing my diamonds, Rader. They are a girl's best friend."

Stubbornness made her carry the charade further. Fancy widened her eyes into what she hoped was a beguiling look. If he expected her to be a second Mona, then perhaps she should let him believe it. Anything was acceptable if it gained her some time. Being here with him, this close, was too much to deal with just now. She needed time to think.

Her charade was rewarded by the tightening of his mouth in renewed anger. Rader flung her hand away as if it offended him and she took advantage of the opportunity to escape.

Turning quickly, she ran out the door and up the stairs, striding quickly toward her room. She would not think about the man she'd left standing in the kitchen, or of his opinion of her. It had been a mistake to come here, but there was nowhere else to go now.

The sound of her door slamming echoed through the house, drowning out the sound of the agonized sob caught in her throat.

Chapter Three

Morning dawned warm and bright. Sunlight streamed through Fancy's window, calling to her sleep-drugged mind insistently. Groaning with unrelieved weariness, she burrowed deeper into the down pillows, closing her eyes tightly against the too-bright invasion.

The tap at her door was faint at first, and she ignored it, willing sleep to return. As if from a distance, she heard the door open quietly. She lay on her stomach, the sheet and blanket a tangle about her as evidence of her restless night.

"Fancy." Rader's voice caressed her senses.

"Mummmm," she mumbled into her pillow.

"Breakfast is nearly ready." Fancy realized Rader was now standing at her bedside. There was no avoiding him.

With an audible sigh, Fancy resigned herself to rejoining the living. A twitch of her nose told her Rader had brought a cup of coffee. Fancy rolled onto her back, the covers sliding about her.

"How can morning be here already?" Her voice was husky with sleep, its normally low tone almost hoarse. With her eyes still closed, she clasped the sheet to her chest and sat up, her hair sliding over her shoulders and across her breast. She brushed its length back absently, combing her fingers through its tangles.

She forced her heavy eyes to open and again take in the simple elegance of the room before bringing her attention around to the tall man standing beside the bed.

Rader was dressed in faded casualness, worn jeans molded to hard thighs, encasing his slim hips. His plaid long-sleeved shirt was equally faded, the sleeves folded back over corded forearms, the neck open to disclose a dark thatch of hair across his chest. Rader held out a mug of steaming coffee, and Fancy accepted it gratefully.

As she tucked the sheet beneath her arms, Fancy sipped the black brew and felt its heat spread through her. A smile curved her lips. "Thanks."

The bed shifted as Rader sat on the end of it. Fancy raised her knees to rest her arms across them, holding the mug carefully in one hand. Rader sat with one leg bent, his other foot on the floor. His dark gaze studied her disheveled appearance, touching the faint shadows that remained beneath her eyes in spite of ten hours in bed.

"I remember a few mornings you brought me coffee in bed."

Fancy glanced at him to better measure the nuances behind his statement. "Quite a few mornings you looked like something the cat dragged in."

"True. I was bent on making some kind of record in riotous living then." He grinned charmingly. "If I remember correctly, you gave me a lecture about that."

"I was young and infatuated."

Something indefinable flickered in his dark gaze. "Yeah, I suppose so."

Fancy studied Rader a moment over her cup, failing to put definition to his tone.

"You don't look as though you slept well. Strange bed?"

She brushed at her tangled hair ineffectually in a self-conscious gesture. "It's so quiet here and so dark. The lack of sound kept waking me, I guess." She didn't lie well and knew he didn't believe her.

Fancy became uncomfortable as Rader continued studying her. It was as if he weighed something in his mind, trying to come to a conclusion about her. She didn't like the feeling. It was something like squirming on the point of a pin and being examined at length by some scientist about to decide her fate.

"You'll find it a quiet life here. I usually work all day, sometimes into the evening. When Mrs. Sartin comes in to do the housekeeping and light cooking, she goes about her work on her own."

Fancy took another sip of coffee. "I can't imagine you living such a tranquil existence." A glint of humor lit her pale eyes and her mouth turned up stiffly. "Let's see, weren't you involved in a legal action

brought against a certain female film star by her
neighbors? Something about a party getting out of
hand and the guests going on an uncontrolled scav-
enger hunt through the neighborhood, I think. And
wasn't there something about the management can-
celing your reservations when a rejected lover staged
a sit-in in the lobby of a prestigious Hollywood
hotel?''

The humor in her eyes turned to a mocking glint as
she fought his attraction with caustic words. ''My,
you'd think they'd be more understanding, especially
for R. C. Malone.'' The process of taking another sip
of coffee hid the teasing curl of her lips. ''And, wasn't
there a paternity suit thrown in there somewhere? I
assume you outdanced that little inconvenience, too?
You are such a clever fellow.''

Rader's wolfish grin revealed almost too-perfect
teeth. ''You know that was foolishness, the meat of
lies that pulp tabloids feed upon. Are you always so
caustic in the morning or is it just me who brings out
the beast in you?''

Something in his look made Fancy overly conscious of the fact that the oversize T-shirt she wore was
an inadequate cover. Rader Malone in person was
every bit as potent as the man lauded by newspapers
and magazines as the sexiest novelist around. The fact
that he was only in his thirties and single just en-
hanced his attractiveness to the press—especially the
female portion of the media.

Fancy had followed his career closely, dreaming of
him, wondering how different things might have been
if they'd met on their own. Instead, they'd been

thrown together into a stew of very explosive emotions in a marriage doomed to disaster.

She'd come to settle those dreams, to rid herself once and for all of those foolish childhood fantasies. But the instant she'd seen him, Fancy had known it was going to take more than spending a few days in his house to erase them.

Fancy automatically took refuge in derision. "It must be the result of that horrendous bus ride yesterday. At times I wondered if I hadn't been taken on a ride to nowhere. I'd have thought this place more accessible by now."

She could sense his withdrawal and felt sad. She liked the excitement of sparring verbally with him, the courting of danger in case he discovered how much she was drawn to him. But she had to keep this distance between them or be entangled forever in the web of his sensual charm.

"I purposely keep this place 'remote' because of those stories you quoted. Too many people happily read and believe them. Anyone who is in the limelight at all is considered fair game for anyone and everyone out for a quick headline or a quick dollar."

Fancy shrugged, unwilling to meet his gaze. He made her feel guilty for quoting those stupid charges that had made good copy in the scandal sheets. She'd known they couldn't be true.

"Here I can work in peace, without interruption, and I can work the hours I choose. There isn't a photographer or reporter hiding behind every tree." He studied her a long moment. "How much do you remember from when you lived here?"

"You've changed the inside a lot."

"On purpose."

"Why?"

His dark eyes measured her. "I have memories, too, that I wanted to ... eradicate ... by making the atmosphere different. You didn't answer the question. What do you remember about being here?"

"I worked at forgetting," Fancy said, brushing aside the very memories he wanted to know. "Is the isolation the only reason you like being here?"

His gaze raked over her again as if he doubted she could ever understand his reasoning. "There's something about the strength of the mountains, their ruggedness—well, as pretentious as it may sound, they fill a need inside me. I can come here and find something that refuels me, smooths the ragged edges."

Fancy was forced to look at him and she was caught by the faraway look on his face. As Rader talked, he leaned back on the bed, resting on one elbow and concentrating on something outside her window. "Here I can get on a horse and ride all day and not pass the same place twice. I can walk where possibly no one has walked for perhaps a hundred years, touch trees that are more than eighty years old, drink from clear creeks that are as pure as the day they were created. I can't think of another place on earth where I can find those things."

This was a side of Rader that Fancy had never seen. A side she hadn't even considered. She studied Rader's serious face. This was a strange discussion to be having at midmorning with this man.

"All that seems in complete opposition to everything I know about you. I see you as the consummate sophisticate. The sensualist. Who is the real Rader Malone?" She set her half-empty coffee cup aside. "The three-piece suit and briefcase version? Or this man seated on my bed in boots and jeans? I don't remember such casual clothing being a part of your wardrobe."

If possible, his eyes darkened. "And I don't remember this lithe, curvacious creature sitting in front of me." The husky undertones were back in his voice, alerting her senses. "The freckles have turned to creamy, flawless skin, the too-wide mouth now generously soft, those strange pale eyes masked and intriguing, hiding all kinds of secrets."

Fancy sat still as Rader reached out and caught a strand of her hair between his fingers. "Saffron. Those straw-yellow braids have turned to silken gold that makes a man want to bury his hands in it." He let the strands slide back against her shoulder. "We have a lot to learn about one another, Fancy."

She moved uncomfortably beneath his scrutiny. "Yeah, I guess we do." She ran long fingers through her loose hair nervously.

She closed her eyes as a mixture of frustration and unwilling awareness of the pull of Rader's attractiveness warred inside her.

"I made a mistake in coming here," Fancy stated. "If you'll take me back to town . . ."

"No. I think we both know why you're here. There is . . . something . . . between us. There always has been."

His eyes held hers compellingly. "You never were one to run away from things. Why start now?"

"I'm not," Fancy said softly.

"Perhaps it would be a greater mistake not to see it through."

Fancy threw her head back in an attempt to escape his assessing gaze.

Rader gritted his teeth in frustration. There were a lot of things being said, but little of any consequence. They were both dancing lightly around a dangerous admission. Was his attraction to her reciprocated, or was she here just to wait out the settlement of her mother's estate? Was she here to...extort something from him? Money? Something else? How much was she like Mona and how much was she like the captivating young girl he'd known ten years ago?

As badly as he wanted to just let the rest go, take her in his arms and make love to her right here in this bed, he couldn't risk it. No matter how she seemed right now, she was Mona's daughter. And if he'd had any doubt of that, seeing her in The Blue Note had confirmed her heritage. Her sensuality hadn't faded one whit, even if she did appear tired and more than a little evasive every time he came near her—physically or emotionally.

A silent struggle was taking place inside Fancy. She sought to control the convulsive gripping of her hands on the sheet. She wanted so badly to just give it all up. Either tell him the truth and take her chances, or find a way out of here to return to San Francisco and try to work. But the need to know for certain that whether what she felt for him might be something valid held her here.

Rader studied her, wondering what was going on behind those golden eyes. The tension in her was clearly evident. The knuckles of her hands were white. If possible, her face had paled even more. There was so much—good and bad—between them. Things that had to be talked out. Things that might permanently affect them both. Things that had to be explored slowly and with care.

So for now, he would let Fancy, and himself, off the hook. He knew when he'd pushed enough. After all, he didn't want her to find a way to get back to the bus station before they'd settled things between them. They had all summer to learn more about the adult versions of each other. They could afford to give themselves some time.

"Well, how about getting dressed and coming down for breakfast? I don't promise anything extravagant, unless you're talented in the area of haute cuisine yourself."

He had deliberately lightened the mood and Fancy was grateful. She allowed herself a small, nervous laugh. "Hardly. Toast and coffee are more my style."

The mocking tone crept back into his voice. "I'd have thought Mona's taste somewhat richer."

Fancy ignored the taunt, reaching again for her cup of cooling coffee. The thin material of her T-shirt stretched and became almost transparent. His breath caught involuntarily. She was an absolutely exquisite creature.

"If you'll excuse me," she said, "I'll shower and be down in a few minutes."

After a long moment, during which he got his breathing back under control, Rader stood. Fancy could feel his dark gaze upon her, but she kept her face averted, concentrating upon the simple process of settling her bedclothes about her again. It took all her willpower to assume a nonchalant attitude with him watching her like that.

Finally, Rader strode briskly from the room and Fancy wilted against her pillows in relief.

In the shower a few minutes later, Fancy turned slowly beneath the stinging cascade. She luxuriated in the feel of it upon her skin. She was a sensual, responsive woman, sensitive to the subtleties of emotion and circumstance. The emotions coming to life between herself and Rader disturbed her in many ways. She naturally sought the emotional tug of war between them, the testing of emotional waters. But intellectually, she knew it was a dangerous game to play.

Far too much was at stake. Her future happiness was pinned upon what happened during her short time with Rader. But what if it didn't work? What if they only hurt each other?

Throwing her head back, Fancy let the water caress her face. Mona. Mona Connors. It always came back to Mona. Rich, beautiful, gadfly Mona. Her relationships with men were shallow, and she easily left them behind. Her marriage to Kurt Malone was a throwaway, apparently. Mona had chosen to ignore it because she'd adopted the name Connors again. What a legacy she'd left. Upon her only daughter had fallen the mantle of an all-for-money reputation, insincerity, disloyalty, vanity and selfishness.

It didn't matter that Fancy had struggled all her life to free herself from her mother's influence. No matter what she said or did, Rader would always be cautious with her because of Mona.

Fancy turned off the water with her foot. Not only was there the emotional entanglement involved between herself and Rader, there was the legal mess of Mona's estate and what was left of Kurt's estate. And the money, or lack of it, was a prime consideration for her.

She smiled, thinking of the challenge Brian Carter was undertaking in untangling the mess of Mona's estate. Fancy just hoped he was half the attorney Rader believed he was. Brian would need every bit of his expertise to accomplish this task. Fancy grew grim again as she was reminded of the immediacy of the problems her lack of funds precipitated.

When she finished drying off, Fancy pulled a fresh pair of jeans and another T-shirt from her duffel bag. Slipping the shirt over her head, she smoothed rumpled denims over slim hips before pulling on socks and pushing on scuffed boots. Brushing her hair took longer.

Normally she braided its length to control it while she slept, but last night it had been too much trouble to do so. It took some time to get the tangles out. Securing it with a band, she allowed her hair to hang free down her back. Now, to face Rader again.

As Fancy descended the stairs, the aroma of sausages mixed with freshly perked coffee reminded Fancy of how hungry she was. Rader stood at the stove, somehow managing not to look out of place. At her entrance, he flashed an assessing glance in her direction. "I was about to send this to the garbage disposal and let you fend for yourself. Will you fix the toast?"

At her nod, Rader dished up sausages and deftly broke eggs into the skillet. His gaze fell over her as Fancy pushed the bread down in the toaster, hesitating slightly on the words Musicians Do It With Grace Notes stenciled across her shirt.

"Doesn't that duffel bag hold anything but jeans and stenciled T-shirts?"

Fancy kept her eyes riveted to the toaster. "It holds what I own."

His eyes narrowed at her dry response. She was lying for some reason. She had to be. Mona's wardrobe had been the central focus of her life. He'd seen some of the bills for it and they'd been astronomical.

In fact, the money Mona had spent on clothes had instigated one of the worst arguments he and Kurt had ever had, widening appreciably the breach between them. Once again, Rader made the resolution to get to the bottom of what made Fancy Connors tick.

Chapter Four

Fancy concentrated on the food, knowing Rader was studying her.

"Are you working on a new book?" Fancy asked to break the silence.

"Umm-hum," Rader said over his coffee cup. "I'm working against a deadline."

"Do you like writing?" Asking questions gave her an excuse to study him.

His even gaze met hers. "Yes, surprisingly. When I was in college, I'd never have guessed my life would turn out this way."

Fancy sipped at her coffee. And I never thought mine would turn out like this, she thought. She stared out the window at the bright sunshine that washed the valley, then noticed a faded blue car coming down the long drive.

"There's Miriam."

"I never knew her first name," Fancy commented. "She was always Mrs. Sartin."

"It's only the last year that I've had permission to use her first name," Rader smiled. "Guess I've proved myself."

Fancy smiled, tense inside at meeting the woman again.

Miriam Sartin was a thin, gray-haired woman with a somewhat hawkish face and piercing blue eyes. She bustled in, put her purse inside a lower cabinet and tossed a blue sweater over the back of a chair.

"Hello, Francine. It's good to see you again."

Fancy relaxed a little. "Thank you. It's good to be here."

Miriam poured herself a cup of coffee and sat down with them. "Things have changed a lot since you left home."

Home. Fancy felt a smile tug at the corner of her mouth. For the first time, she could say that word and feel it was right. Even though she'd been here only a short time, and not quite a happy time, this *was* home.

"Fancy wasn't here long enough for this to be home, Miriam."

The woman's sharp glance flicked from Rader to Fancy. "Oh, I don't know. It doesn't take long to know whether somethin' fits."

"Well, I'll leave you two ladies to catch up, then," Rader said as he stood. "I have work to do."

Fancy felt the tension unwind a little inside her when Rader left the kitchen. She sipped at her cooled coffee because she wasn't sure what to do or say next.

Miriam stood, taking her coffee cup with her. "And I've got things to do, too. My son is bringing some vegetables by on his way to work. I plan to fix some of them for tonight's dinner. You remember Paul, don't you?"

"Yes. He may not remember me."

"I told him you were coming." Mrs. Sartin tied on an apron. "Here, let me warm that coffee for you." Before Fancy could protest, Miriam had dumped out the cold contents and poured a fresh cup of coffee. "There, now."

"Where is Paul working?" Fancy remembered a blond-haired boy who was always into some kind of mischief.

"In Eureka Springs. A tour guide. You remember the place. Full of old houses and funny little shops? Well, most of the old houses are restored, some turned into bed-and-breakfast places, and the funny little shops are full of tourists now. Paul works there summers. Earns money for college."

"What's Sharon doing?"

"Oh, she's got a real good job at the bank. Due for a promotion to vice president. She and Rader have been seein' one another for some time now. I expect an announcement before too long."

Fancy tried to imagine Sharon Sartin and Rader together. Sharon had always been different. Everything she did had to be just a little better than anyone else. She had been a cheerleader, class president, homecoming queen. There was always a haughty air about the dark-haired girl.

Now Fancy recognized that Sharon had to feel superior as a way of competing. Back then, it had just irked Fancy that the girl had looked down her nose at her from the superior position of being four years older. And now she had Rader, too. What was the old saying? Them that has, gets?

Fancy watched Mrs. Sartin clear the pans and plates and run a sink full of sudsy water. "I was surprised when Rader said you were coming."

"It was good of him to invite me," Fancy said, turning the coffee cup round and round on the table.

"I was sorry to hear about Mona."

Fancy flicked a glance at the woman and met her speculative gaze. "You don't have to be kind, Mrs. Sartin. I know what my mother was and I didn't like it any better than most everyone else."

Something changed in the woman's look. "Must have been hard for you."

"What? Living with her? Or living in her shadow?"

"No need to be sarcastic with me."

Fancy smiled. "Thanks, Mrs. Sartin."

"For what?"

"Treating me like a human being. So many people have tiptoed around me the last couple of weeks. All except Rader, of course."

"No love lost there," the woman commented, washing the few dishes.

"No. And I understand his feelings. He blames Mona for Kurt's death."

"No need to rehash old stories."

Again Fancy managed a smile. "Thanks. Again."

"Rader's been awfully good to us over the years. After my man died, I needed to work. Rader was home for a while that spring and heard about it. Phoned and asked me to keep house for him." She shrugged. "Most normal thing to me. I'd kept house for my family for years. This wasn't much different." She glanced around the kitchen. "Bigger place. A lot fancier. But, Rader's not a fancy kind of man."

You could say that again, Fancy thought, smiling at the double meaning that could be derived from the woman's statement.

"He's done a lot for folks around here. Why, when one of those pictures was going to be made from one of his books, he suggested they film it here in the valley. Took all one summer and put a lot of people to work. Extra money when times were bad. People remember that. And instead of lettin' those Hollywood folks run over things, he made sure they didn't. They put things back just the way they were," she nodded with satisfaction. "And he's kept this place going. Bought more land, runs horses and cattle, you know."

Once again Fancy felt she was in over her head. This was another side to Rader. A side she liked. He obviously cared for the people in the valley. She'd seen a hint of that sensitive side when he'd sent Brian to take care of Mona's funeral arrangements and any legal problems there might be connected with her death. She'd resented his intrusion on one hand, but had been grateful for it on another.

"I was surprised he kept the house," Fancy said.

"Oh, Rader loves this house. Wouldn't part with it for anything."

Just then a roar announced Paul's arrival. He spun the motorcycle in a circle, then braked in a cloud of dust.

"That boy, that boy," Mrs. Sartin commented, shaking her head while drying her hands on a dish towel. "He rides that thing like a crazy man."

The back door opened with a bang and a young man of medium height and stocky build came in, pulling a helmet off his head.

"Hey, Mom, here's the veggies you wanted. The green beans are about finished."

"Thank goodness. I've snapped and canned enough to feed Cox's army."

Then Paul's gaze lit upon Fancy. "Francine!" He threw himself into a chair opposite her and grinned impishly. "The last time I saw you, I pulled your ponytail and you screeched like a banshee."

"Ha! I remember you trying to scalp me!" Fancy laughed. Paul was a breath of fresh air.

Paul glanced at his mother. "Now would I do a thing like that?"

"Yes, you would," Miriam said, ruffling his hair as she set a cup of coffee in front of him.

"Your mother said you worked in Eureka Springs," Fancy said.

"Yeah. I'm a guide. It's turned into quite a tourist mecca since you were last there. All kinds of art galleries, a Christmas shop, Victorian houses. And then there's the Passion Play."

Fancy remembered the Passion Play. It was a reenactment of the last days of Christ before the crucifixion. Though it was a well-known event during the spring, summer and fall, Fancy had never seen it. Mona had thought it "quaint" and ignored all her requests to go.

"I've got tomorrow off. Why don't I give you a little tour of the area?"

"I'd like that, if it's not too much trouble."

"Not at all. Uh, the only vehicle I have is my bike, though."

His look was not quite apologetic. More proud.

"That thing?" Fancy grinned, studying it through the window. "A lean, mean machine with liquid-cooled DOHC 498 cc eight-valve four-stroke in-line twin engine, hard-stopping front disc brakes with exclusive balanced actuation caliper, box-section perimeter frame, hydraulic fork matched by a super rear suspension," she recited evenly, watching Paul's expression out of the corner of her eye.

"Whooeee! You got one?"

"Nope. But a friend of mine does and loves it probably as much as you do yours. I was privileged to be on the back of it."

"Great!" Paul glanced at his watch and jumped to his feet. "Got to run. I'll be here about nine tomorrow and we'll do the sights."

"I'll be ready."

With a wave, Paul was out the door. A second later, he roared down the drive, performing a wheelie just before going out of sight.

"That boy, that boy," Mrs. Sartin murmured fondly. "He gives me white hair, but I don't know what I'd do without him. He helps me with our large garden and does all the outside work at home."

"He's not changed much," Fancy commented. "I remember he always did everything at break-neck speed. One day, he ran down the center aisle of the classroom and did a perfect slide up to the teacher's desk. She wasn't impressed, but the rest of us were."

"No wonder I couldn't keep the knees and seat in his jeans." Miriam laughed.

Fancy went over to the sink and watched as Mrs. Sartin began unloading the sack of vegetables Paul had delivered.

"It's been a long time since I had fresh green beans."

A head of lettuce, new carrots and potatoes went into the sink to be washed, and pea pods went into a pan.

"If you've got nothing else to do, why don't you shell these peas."

Fancy looked at the pan. "I—I don't know how," she had to admit.

Mrs. Sartin glanced up at her. "Don't know how?" She shrugged her thin shoulders. "Well, I can't say I'm surprised. Mona didn't know where the kitchen was and wasn't about to find out."

Fancy winced at the comparison but watched as the older woman showed her how to split the pod with her thumb nail and spill out the peas. Ten minutes later she was seated on a stool at the counter and had half the pan shelled.

After that was finished, she helped Mrs. Sartin prepare the new potatoes and carrots and start a roast for dinner that evening. As she worked, Mrs. Sartin talked about how long the roast should cook, how to test the vegetables for doneness and decided aloud whether to prepare lemon-meringue pie or banana cream for dessert.

Before Fancy realized it, the afternoon was nearly gone. When Mrs. Sartin left at four, Fancy was in charge of finishing dinner and getting it on the table. That was fine, but she didn't look forward to sharing a meal alone with Rader.

But she didn't have to share it alone. Promptly at six, the door bell rang. Fancy waited, not certain whether to answer it or leave it for Rader. Then she heard Rader's footsteps hurrying to the door. She waited just inside the kitchen door, uncertain whether to announce dinner or not.

"Come in," Rader said. Then there was a long silence before Fancy heard another voice.

"What a day! I'm ready for something cool."

"I'm sure I can find something."

Fancy stepped back from the door and busied herself with checking the vegetables simmering on the stove.

"I wondered where you'd hidden all day," Rader said as he came into the kitchen.

"I wasn't hiding. I was helping Mrs. Sartin."

Rader's eyebrows lifted in open skepticism. "Helping? How?"

She indicated the food. "Dinner. When will you be ready to eat?"

Rader's surprise turned to a frown. "You're not here as a . . . servant."

Fancy shrugged. "I'm glad to help out. Gives me something to do. Is your guest staying?"

"Yes, Sharon is staying."

"Sharon?"

"Sharon Sartin."

"I see."

"Still jealous?"

"Jealous? I was never jealous of Sharon," Fancy lied, turning away. "She never had anything I wanted."

"Thirty minutes," was Rader's short reply as he walked out with two glasses.

The urge to stick her tongue out pricked at Fancy, but she only stirred the vegetables. At the moment, she wasn't certain whether she was expected to eat with them or should plan on eating in the kitchen. She wanted to hide, as Rader called it, in the kitchen. But some imp inside made her set another plate at the dining table.

Promptly thirty minutes later, Fancy dished up the roast and vegetables, with the pickles Mrs. Sartin had been so proud of putting up herself. The tea was poured and coffee was perking to be served with the lemon-meringue pie Fancy had learned to make that afternoon.

The table looked nice and she was admiring it when Rader and Sharon strolled in, arm in arm.

"Why, Francine," Sharon said, sweeping Fancy head to toe with a studying gaze. "How nice to see you again."

Sharon might have been speaking to a child. Then Fancy remembered that she hadn't changed all day, and her shirt and jeans bore the evidence of her kitchen labors. Suddenly she was conscious that her hair was escaping from its braid and that she should have washed her face.

Sharon, of course, looked perfect in a lemon-colored shirtwaist that was fresh and cool, with her dark hair drawn up in a charmingly loose style that framed her oval face. Her arm was hooked through Rader's possessively, and her smile evidenced her self-assurance.

"Dinner is ready," Fancy said, deciding she would eat in the kitchen, after all.

"Thanks," Rader said, pulling back a chair for Sharon.

Then he moved to do the same for Fancy.

"Uh, I—I won't be joining you," she stammered, wishing she'd realized earlier that she couldn't watch Rader and Sharon together.

"Of course, you are," Rader said, pulling out the chair. "You spent all day helping prepare this. Now you'll enjoy it."

"Francine helped with the meal? How...nice," Sharon said, unfolding her napkin.

Then something clicked in Fancy's mind. Sharon was acting exactly like Mona. There was the same possessive glow in her eyes when she looked at Rader, and the same disdain for those who put their hands to work. Fancy sank into her chair, avoiding Rader's look.

"Well, Francine, Rader tells me you're taking a little vacation. Vacation from what?"

Fancy concentrated on spooning out potatoes and carrots. "This and that."

"What do you mean?" Sharon frowned.

"Just that I'm not involved in anything at the moment," which was the truth. "When Rader invited me to stay here for a while, I thought it would be...fun...to come back and see how things have changed."

"And have they?"

"You remember, don't you?"

"I was never here...when you lived here," Sharon admitted, with a sideways glance at Rader.

"Well, it has changed a little. Rader's done quite a bit of redecorating. And Paul tells me Eureka Springs had become quite a tourist center."

"Oh, yes. He works there in the summer—" she waved a hand in dismissal "—some little guide job."

"Don't you know what he does?" Fancy suspected Sharon was still interested in little outside herself.

"I know he shows people through the Victorian houses, but he's always got something going. I can't keep up with him." Sharon sipped at her iced tea. "You should go to Eureka and see how it's changed."

"Paul's taking me on a tour tomorrow," Fancy commented, passing Rader the pickles.

"He is?" Rader seemed surprised.

"Umm-hum. He was here this morning, delivering the vegetables."

"Paul has quite a green thumb."

"Does he? Your mother said he helped her with the garden and did the outside work."

"He's always grubbing in the dirt," Sharon interjected.

"What do you do?" Fancy asked. "Your mother said you worked in a bank?"

"Yes. In the investment department."

"I didn't remember you being interested in math in school."

"I wasn't. I only discovered my talent for investment analysis while in college in Springfield. Rader, have you thought more about those bonds I recommended?"

"I haven't talked to Brian yet," Rader responded.

From then through dessert, the conversation bounced back and forth between Rader and Sharon, and Fancy was glad of it. By the time dessert was over, her stomach was hurting from the stress and from not taking her medication, and she gratefully retreated to the kitchen.

A short time later, she heard Rader and Sharon leave the dining room, and she cleared the table. But before she was finished in the kitchen, Rader pushed through the swinging door.

"I won't have you being kitchen help while you're here."

"I enjoy helping Mrs. Sartin."

Rader leaned against the cabinet, facing Fancy. "That's fine, but I won't have you playing Cinderella."

"Oh? Who's playing the wicked stepsister?" As if it isn't obvious, she thought. But this time Sharon will win the prince. She has the invitation to the ball, issued by the prince himself.

"You and Sharon never got along, did you?"

"We didn't exactly run in the same crowd. She was a senior in high school when I left. She always had her eye on you, though."

Rader studied her a moment. "I don't remember that."

Fancy didn't like remembering it so well.

"Isn't Sharon going to be wondering where you are?"

"She's not my keeper," Rader commented. "I just came for more iced tea."

"Here. I'll fix it," Fancy said, her hands colliding with his as they reached for the glasses. "Sorry."

"Somehow we do keep bumping into one another, don't we?"

Fancy glanced up to meet his dark gaze. She never could read what was on Rader's mind, but at times like tonight, she wasn't sure she wanted to know. Slowly she released a glass. "I'm going upstairs."

"Perhaps you should," he said.

Chapter Five

Fancy had just finished a breakfast of toast and coffee when Paul arrived in a cloud of dust. She quickly swallowed one of the pills the doctor had prescribed for her ulcer when Paul burst in the back door.

"Ready?"

She picked up her shoulder bag as Rader strode into the kitchen.

"Hey, Rader! How's the new book going?"

"Slow," Rader said, pouring himself another cup of coffee.

"Fancy and I are going to Eureka Springs. I'm showing her the sights."

"Are you," was Rader's dry comment.

Fancy saw his mouth tighten momentarily and wondered what was bothering him now. She'd gone upstairs after dinner last night and relaxed in a fragrant tub of hot water, reading a book she found on her night stand, then went to bed. She heard Sharon leave around eleven and Rader come upstairs a short time later. She'd held her breath, hoping Rader wouldn't come to see if she was awake, but he'd gone directly to his room. She was both disappointed and relieved and hated that he made her feel either way.

"Any problem with that?" Fancy asked.

"None." Rader shrugged. "This is your vacation."

"Okay." She turned to Paul. "I guess I'm ready to go."

"Great. See you later, Rader." Paul waved and followed Fancy out the door.

Rader watched them from the window, sipping slowly at his coffee. Paul got on the motorcycle and Fancy mounted behind him, her long legs balancing on the ground until Paul was set. Tucking her long hair up, she slipped on the extra helmet Paul handed her, then slid her arms around his waist. Rader winced inwardly, feeling a stab of jealousy he didn't want to feel. For the tenth time, he asked himself why he'd invited her to stay the summer.

But he knew the answer. He'd wanted to see her again. Wanted to find out what she was like; how much like Mona she was. Fancy laughed at something Paul said, and Rader's gut tightened. She was like Mona. With a quirk of her finger, men came running. He turned on his heel and strode out of the kitchen, letting the swinging door bang against the wall.

Fancy loved riding the cycle. She felt free with the wind beating against her face, the beauty of the

Ozarks surrounding her. She'd forgotten how ruggedly handsome the land was with its big oaks and limestone cliffs embracing the highway. In short time, they were entering Eureka Springs. The train was leaving the station, carrying tourists on a short scenic tour, but Paul swept past and into the main part of town.

He parked the bike on a main street, and they began their walking tour. By noon they'd visited most of the sites including the Christmas Shop, bookstores and a Victorian house.

"How about an ice cream?"

"Sounds great," Fancy said.

Later they wandered down the street, licking cones, toward the city park. A crowd was gathering, and they stopped to see what was happening.

There was a small temporary stage set up and several men with guitars. A bass player and a banjo player sat on wooden chairs, tuning their instruments.

Intrigued, Fancy watched as one of the guitarists started picking a tune. One by one, the others joined in until they had a rousing rendition of a tune that Fancy didn't recognize. With tapping feet and gentle smiles, they seemed to communicate without words, moving from one tune to another without direction. Fancy finished her cone and found herself clapping to a beat along with the growing crowd.

As the band played, Fancy moved forward, pushing through the crowd as she listened until she was in the front row. Paul followed.

"They're pretty good, aren't they?" Paul said.

"Very. Do they play here all the time?"

"No." He shrugged. "Whenever two or three of them get together, they play. There's usually something going on."

Fancy listened, recognizing bits and pieces of old English melodies that were either part of a new rendition or changed by the addition of the banjo.

"That sounds like 'Greensleeves,'" Fancy commented. "The one before that was... Oh, I can't remember it."

Paul studied her rapt expression. "Do you play?"

Fancy shrugged, her gaze on the musicians. "Some." She did play. Had for years. And she missed it terribly.

Before she realized what he was doing, Paul stepped forward and caught the attention of the guitarist. "Charlie, can Fancy join in?"

"Sure thing."

"Oh, no..." Fancy started.

"Could she borrow your guitar?"

"No, Paul." Fancy grabbed at his arm.

"Sure. I could use a break."

Charlie handed Fancy the instrument.

"Here," Paul said.

"I—I can't," Fancy said, glancing around at the crowd.

"Sure you can. Let's see what you can do."

By this time, the others were urging her up on the stage. Fancy really wanted to play, but felt she was intruding.

"Go on," Paul pushed Fancy forward.

Refusing would create a bigger scene than doing what she really wanted to do, so Fancy stepped up on the stage.

"You go ahead," she told the other guitarist. "I'll join in when I can."

They were four bars into a song before Fancy began strumming the strings of the borrowed guitar, and before the song was finished she was playing right along with the others. By the third song, she was taking the lead occasionally and loving every minute of it.

Paul was watching from the front row, shouting and clapping encouragement. Once, when Fancy had full control of a tune, the others dropped back and let her take a solo. Joy flooded through her as she held the instrument and felt the music flow into her fingers. The encouraging smiles of the other musicians supported her efforts to modulate the music into another key and improvise, and she felt the warmth of oneness. It was like really coming home, and it was with reluctance that she handed the guitar back to Charlie and stepped off the stage to applause.

"Join us anytime, gal. Anytime."

"Thanks." She smiled, pleasure coloring her cheeks.

"You're really good," Paul said, hugging her close. "Really good."

"You shouldn't have pushed me into that," she chided.

"But you enjoyed it, didn't you?"

She laughed, linking her arm with his as they walked out of the park. "I loved it."

"Where's your guitar?"

"Back in San Francisco. In storage. I'm not really sure where. Rader's attorney took care of things."

"Miss it?"

Fancy's smile was rueful. "Very."

"They liked you. And they don't take to strangers much."

"I wish I knew the tunes they were playing."

"They're mountain tunes. 'Silver Needles,' and you recognized 'Greensleeves,' then there was 'The Orange Blossom Special,' and some I don't even know the names of. Tunes that have been handed down through father and son for a century."

"They're beautiful. Some haunting. Some joyous. They...lilt across the heart and touch the soul."

"Ummm, you're a born musician," Paul said. "Only someone born to it talks about it like they're making love."

Fancy gave Paul a playful punch. "Oh, you!"

"What kind of music do you play?"

"Classical guitar."

"You've obviously been trained."

"I've had a few lessons," she admitted, wishing Paul wouldn't ask any more questions. The Sartin family was far too close to Rader.

"Hungry?"

Fancy glanced at her watch. "Wow! I didn't realize how late it was getting. You probably need to get back...."

"This is my day off, remember?"

"And you've spent it showing me around. Just like you were working. I'm sorry."

"I've enjoyed every minute of it. Especially when you were up there with Charlie, Gage, Ben and the others. But now I'm hungry. How does barbecue ribs sound?"

"Fantastic!" Fancy enthused. "I haven't had a good rib...since I left."

"Not on Mona's menu?"

"Not in San Francisco," Fancy responded.

Thirty minutes later, they were elbow-deep in barbecue sauce, with a side of potato salad and slaw, followed by the most delicious vanilla ice cream with fresh strawberries Fancy had ever eaten.

"I am stuffed," Fancy complained, leaning back.

"You must have not eaten in years," Paul said with a laugh, noting the pile of rib bones on her plate.

"I was a pig, wasn't I?"

"These are the best ribs around," Paul said. "No one gets out of here without eating too much."

"I need to walk."

"Then let's walk."

Paul paid the bill and followed Fancy outside.

"I—I'm sorry I didn't bring any money," Fancy apologized, wishing she'd had some to bring.

"Today is my treat," Paul assured her.

They walked down the street in the late afternoon sun, full of good food and feeling pleasantly companionable. Fancy didn't know when she'd enjoyed a day so much. It had been a long time. Far too long.

By the time they drove down Rader's drive, it was growing dark. There were lights on in the kitchen and in the living room. Fancy entered the house through the kitchen door, hoping to get upstairs to shower and change without Rader knowing she was home.

But Rader was in the kitchen.

"Fancy."

"Rader." She started through the room.

"You were gone a long time."

Fancy's stomach was beginning to bother her. She shouldn't have eaten the ribs. Certainly not so many. Her doctor had told her she didn't need a controlled diet; just discover what she could and couldn't eat. And take her medication. Well, perhaps barbecue ribs was off her list.

"We had a very good time."

"You and Paul?"

Fancy stopped in front of the swinging door at the tone of Rader's question.

"Yes. Paul and me. Any problem?"

"These are good, decent people."

"Implying what?"

"I don't want them . . . hurt."

"Implying I will hurt them in some way?" Anger narrowed her eyes. "You really don't think much of me, do you?"

"Let's just say I'm . . . warning you. Be careful."

"You're out of line, Rader. . . ."

Rader stepped in front of her. Even with her hair falling around her face, she was beautiful. Her cheeks were flushed with a light sunburn, but her eyes were icy with anger. Unbidden, his gaze dropped to the front of her T-shirt. The Blue Note was stenciled across the front in a fading blue script. It reminded him again of who and what she was.

"Just remember what I said." Then he pushed past her and out of the kitchen.

Fancy went upstairs, took a pill for her stomach and laid down for a while. She stared at the ceiling, thinking about what had happened during the past few weeks. For so long, she'd just shut it all out of her mind because it was too much to think about. It was crazy how it had all happened at once.

First the appendicitis attack at work. Then while she was in the hospital, she'd mentioned the chronic upset stomach and pain she experienced and they'd run some tests. The result? Ulcer. Of course, she should have expected that, but then, she didn't think in terms of failure. And illness meant, to her, a failure to be in control. And she wanted to always be in control.

Then Mona had died. That seemed the greatest irony, considering everything else.

The tap at the door startled her. She sat up and tossed back her hair, but didn't answer. It had to be Rader. There was no one else in the house.

Rader opened the door and leaned against the door frame as if he didn't trust himself in her room again.

"Ignoring me won't work."

"I can try. Might be best for both of us." She wouldn't volunteer to leave. She had no place to go.

"Aren't you going to eat dinner?"

Fancy glanced at the clock on the bedside table. It was seven. "No. Paul and I ate in Eureka Springs."

Irritation firmed his mouth, and his eyes narrowed as he studied her. "Do you feel all right?"

"Of course," she lied. "Why?"

"You were laying down. That . . . doesn't seem like you."

"But you don't know this me."

"I guess not." He straightened. "Well, if you want anything . . ."

"Don't pretend with me, Rader. You're sorry you asked me to come, aren't you?"

Rader studied her at length. "I'm not sure."

"You're afraid I'll corrupt your friends." That had hurt her a lot, but she wasn't going to let Rader know how much. He might use it to his advantage, and he didn't need any more opportunities to make her sorry she'd come. Her dream was empty. She shouldn't have come to try to fill it because now she knew it was empty where before, she'd at least had the hope.

"You're Mona's daughter," he said as if that explained everything.

"I'm also someone else's daughter," she reminded him. "But I'm more myself. Why don't you wait until you know who I am before you decide what I'm not."

Rader didn't say anything for a few minutes, then straightened. "Maybe we need to know more about one another."

"I'd like that opportunity."

With a last lingering glance, Rader turned and carefully closed the door behind him, leaving Fancy sitting in the middle of the bed, staring at the door and wondering if Rader had been apologizing.

Fancy laid back on the bed and tears flooded her eyes. She brushed them away angrily. Tears were surrender, and she would never surrender.

God, how much had changed in ten years. Mona had taken Fancy to San Francisco the year she turned fifteen. Fancy had sulked and argued, but Mona had insisted. Fancy discovered the guitar that year.

She'd taken the class in high school to spite Mona but had discovered a real talent and love for music. She'd taken lessons from the school music teacher until she'd surpassed his abilities. Then he'd suggested she try getting into a school run by a retired internationally-known guitarist.

Alfonso read the note of recommendation from her teacher, then listened to Fancy play. He'd accepted her as a student, complimenting her talent, then named a tuition fee that might as well have been the moon.

So, Fancy lied about her age and got a job playing the dinner show at Rolando's. Providing music had been an experiment for Rolando, but before she finished the week, Fancy was a permanent performer Thursday through Sunday, from 7:00 p.m. to 11:00 p.m. She made enough to pay her tuition and all she could eat. She did her homework on breaks and weekends. Mona assumed she was out with friends and asked no questions.

When Fancy graduated from high school, she began to teach at Alfonso's in addition to taking her own lessons. Her day began with school from eight to noon, lessons from noon to four, and ended with her performance from seven to eleven. She fell into bed exhausted at midnight, usually before Mona got home.

For three years, she rode that merry-go-round, barely able to stay on. Mona didn't create income.

Occasionally she gave Fancy money for rent, but had no idea that rent was a scheduled expense and frequently "forgot" it. Everything Mona got from "friends" went back into her own maintenance.

Then the unthinkable had happened. Mona hadn't been feeling well for weeks when Fancy finally persuaded her to go to the doctor. Several tests later, the verdict was in. Serious. Surgery. Perhaps chemotherapy. They would see.

Mona was inconsolable. She cried and walked the floor for days. Finally, Fancy convinced her to have the surgery.

Once the decision was made, Mona prepared for hospitalization as though preparing for a major performance. By the day of the surgery, she'd become a convincingly tragic, beautiful woman for whom the nurses responded to every whim.

The surgery took longer than expected. Fancy paced and worried. The diagnosis was not good. The surgeons hoped they'd "gotten it all," but . . .

Mona took the pills prescribed, fretted that she lost weight, studied her face and body in the mirror and increased her visits to the hairdresser and the health club, and bought a new wardrobe for her new role.

The bills began coming in. They added up to thousands, with the medication being an on-going expense. Fancy found a third job at The Blue Note.

She sang the early show at The Blue Note every night, barely making it to Rolando's to play her four nights there. For the next eighteen months, her life was a blur. Then she'd collapsed.

The pain in her abdomen had begun in the afternoon, but she'd ignored it. It was different than the dull ache and indigestion she frequently ignored, but she'd told herself it was nothing. By her eight o'clock break, she had to admit something was wrong. But by then, she'd passed out and Rolando had called an ambulance.

Now she was the patient. A very impatient patient. They'd operated for appendicitis, then had run more tests. Anemia and ulcer had been added to her chart.

Two days before she was to be released, Rolando came and told her of Mona's death. Fancy checked herself out of the hospital that afternoon, getting to the apartment just ahead of Brian.

The next week was a nightmare. When Rader arrived for the funeral, Fancy steeled herself for a confrontation. But Rader had been sympathetic and had invited her to come to Arkansas for a vacation.

So, recognizing a way to escape the ever-mounting pressure, she bundled up the bills and wrote promises to pay as soon as Mona's estate was settled. That worked for Mona's bills, but Fancy's own were now long overdue. The pressure was building again.

Fancy rolled over onto her stomach. If Rader knew about her situation, what would he do? Since she arrived, Rader had been confusing. Sometimes she sensed him watching her with suspicion. But sometimes, like today, there was that singing tension between them that made her realize he was very aware of her as a woman.

She knew the tangled webs of Mona's influence still enmeshed his feelings about her. Would she, in the short span of a summer, cut through enough of the lies and deceit of all these years to make a difference? Especially when she had lies of her own to keep hidden?

"Oh, Rader," she whispered into the darkness. "Why couldn't we have just started fresh? Why couldn't you just love me for being me?"

The next day, Fancy managed to get through breakfast without encountering Rader, but as she started back upstairs, Rader came out of his office.

"Brian will be coming today," he announced.

Fáncy stopped with one foot on the bottom step. "Oh? Any particular reason?"

"He's coming to discuss some business with me. I don't know if he has any information about Mona's estate or not."

"I see. Well, when will he be here?"

"In time for dinner. I want you to join us."

She cocked her head to one side. "I'm sure you'll want to talk business."

"In other words, you don't want to have dinner with me."

"We seem to rub each other the wrong way."

"We didn't always."

"I know. But things are different now, aren't they?"

"Are they?"

"I didn't want them to be, but they are."

"What did you want?" His hand rested on the newel post next to her own.

She made herself meet his gaze. "Maybe I wanted to recapture the past. And that was a mistake." An ache developed in her stomach and unconsciously she rested her hand against it. "Maybe I just wanted to see if the Rader Malone I read about in the magazines is anything like the one I knew."

"Is he?"

"I'm not sure. Why did you ask me to come?"

His smile was mocking. "Maybe I wanted to see how much Fancy is like the Francine I knew."

She wouldn't ask if she was because she knew his opinion was colored too much by his dislike for Mona. If he gave her time, maybe she could make him understand that she wasn't Mona, never had been and never would be. The question was, would he give her the chance?

Chapter Six

Brian arrived at four. Fancy was in the kitchen with Mrs. Sartin, getting last-minute instructions. Though Rader had told Fancy he didn't want her serving, she liked being useful. Otherwise, time weighed heavily. She might be on vacation, but she needed to keep busy.

Mrs. Sartin had just left when Rader pushed the kitchen door open. "Brian's here. Would you join us in the den?"

"Okay," Fancy said, wiping her hands on a dish towel.

She followed Rader to one of the rooms she hadn't yet explored. It was paneled with light oak that matched the desk and tables. The fireplace at one end was large, and she thought it would be great to sit in front of in the winter. Except, she wouldn't be there in the winter.

Brian stood in front of the fireplace as if it was a favorite spot for him, also.

"Fancy," he greeted, crossing the room and sticking out his hand. "It's good seeing you again."

She clasped his hand firmly. "Thanks." She glanced at Rader. "Have you any information about Mona's estate?"

"Nope. Nothing yet. It's taking a while to get all the loose ends tied up. Since she died in a crash, the FAA has to investigate and that takes a while. Then there's all the bills to sort out before a final accounting can take place. I haven't found any insurance policies. Did Mona have any?"

"Not that I'm aware of," Fancy admitted, wishing she could have been so lucky.

If settling the estate dragged on, as Brian suggested, then she was going to be in real trouble with the hospital. Fancy erased the frown creasing her forehead and shrugged her shoulders. "Well, I guess I'll just have to wait."

"Maybe it won't be that long," Brian said. "I've got some mail for you."

"You have?"

"Here." Brian handed her a packet with a rubber band around it. "This ought to make the days go a little faster."

Fancy glanced at the packet, then at Rader when she heard him grunt in derision.

"Fashion magazines. Yeah, that ought to keep you busy for a few days." He looked at Brian. "I don't know why she reads them, though. All I've ever seen her wear is those jeans and faded T-shirts."

Brian chuckled, glancing from one to the other. "Hate to tell you but that's all I've ever seen her wear. In fact, that's all she owns, as far as I know."

Fancy looked at Rader and lifted her chin in an I-told-you-so attitude. The magazines were Mona's, but she wasn't about to explain anything to Rader. He seemed to want to believe the worst of her, so let him. If he didn't have any more faith in her than that, then she'd made a big mistake in hoping for any kind of relationship between them.

"If there's nothing more, I'll leave you two to discuss your business."

"Dinner at six?" Rader asked pointedly.

"Six," Fancy repeated, getting the message. He wasn't going to let her hide out in her room tonight.

Fancy turned to leave, but Brian stopped her. "I noticed a couple of envelopes that looked like bills from a hospital. I need to have all the bills—"

"I don't know what they'd be, but if it's something you need, I'll give them to you before you leave."

"Okay." Brian shrugged, glancing at Rader.

After Fancy left, Rader poured Brian a drink. "What was that all about?"

"I'm not sure, but I think our gal is hiding something."

"I've thought that ever since she got here. Find out anything about her or Mona?"

"Very little. Apparently Fancy kept pretty much to herself. And the people at The Blue Note aren't very talkative."

Rader sipped at his Scotch. "They lived in an apartment."

"A small two-bedroom with efficiency kitchen."

"Doesn't sound like Mona."

"Uh...there was something else."

"What?" Rader spun around.

"They did an autopsy on Mona because of the manner of death."

Brian seemed tentative, which was unusual. "And?" Rader prompted.

"She was sick, Rader."

"Sick?"

"Very sick. In fact, she didn't have many more months to live."

"Did she know?" Rader asked before he thought.

"The point is, did Fancy know? And I don't know that she did. Nothing indicates it."

Rader stared out the window, the drink in his hand forgotten. "Keep digging."

"You're sure? I'm not sure I like investigating Fancy."

"Something isn't right and I want to know what it is."

"Why? Because you care about her...more than you want her to know? You think she's out for your money?" Brian shrugged. "She doesn't seem the gold-digging type."

"Mona was."

"But Fancy isn't Mona, is she?"

"That's what I want to know. Before it's too late."

Fancy threw the packet of magazines on the bed and ripped open the white envelope. It wasn't a bill, but it was a letter threatening to turn her account over to a collection agency if acceptable payment terms weren't reached within ten days. The date was ten days prior.

She sank onto the edge of the bed, her shoulders slumping in defeat. She'd tried to make payment arrangements. Or rather, she'd tried to convince the hospital credit office that she would pay them as soon as she could return to work. When they wouldn't accept that, she had tried to get her doctor to release her for work immediately, but he'd refused.

It had been only thirty days since her surgery and with the anemia combined with an ulcer, he'd refused to let her return to work at least another thirty days. It had been then that Fancy had surrendered to the obvious. She couldn't work, she had no money, Mona's estate couldn't be settled, as far as she knew there was no insurance and she had no place to go. Rader's invitation had been a godsend. But it was only a delaying tactic at this point.

Promptly at six, Fancy put dinner on the table and they sat down. Rader was at one end of the table, Brian at the other with Fancy in between. The roast chicken was succulent, the dressing perfectly moist, the fresh green beans tasty, but to Fancy, everything tasted like cardboard.

"Are you feeling all right, Fancy?" Brian asked. "You look a little pale."

"I—I'm fine," she said, and tried to ignore Rader's questioning look.

"Was the envelope a bill?" Brian asked, cutting his chicken studiously.

"No. Just a notice of a magazine subscription lapse."

Rader harumphed and Fancy smiled. Learning about the magazines but knowing she owned nothing but jeans really got to him and it tickled her to know it did.

"This is delicious," Brian said.

"Thanks," Fancy said. "Mrs. Sartin told me what to do, but I prepared it. My very first dinner."

"Congratulations. Who did the cooking for you and Mona?"

Fancy glanced at Rader and resented the skepticism she saw in his face. "We ate out most of the time."

"Who was paying the bills?"

"We paid our own bills." Fancy glared at him.

"Mona always had someone paying the bills."

Fancy laid down her fork very carefully, then looked up at Brian. "Please excuse me. I'll bring in the dessert and let you serve yourself coffee."

Brian started to stand but Fancy waved away the gesture and went into the kitchen. Standing just inside the door, she drew a deep breath and closed her eyes. Why did Rader have to be so cruel? So he hadn't liked Mona. She was dead. There was no reason to keep making hateful remarks about her all the time.

"You were pretty hard on her."

Rader shoved his plate aside. "She gets to me."

"I can see that. The question is why?"

"She's too much like Mona."

"Mona's gone. That's what this is all about. If you hated her so much, why did you send me to help out with the details of the funeral and estate? Why not just leave it for Fancy to take care of herself?"

"I don't know. I guess I just remembered her as a fourteen-year-old kid who had no one."

"Really? Doesn't look like that to me. Looks to me like you're interested in the twenty-four-year-old version."

Rader didn't like the feeling that Brian might be right. When Fancy stepped off that bus, what he'd felt had not been compassion, but passion. Having her in the house, wearing those skintight jeans and faded T-shirts was almost more than his libido could stand sometimes. And when she turned those strange amber eyes on him, it was as if she looked right through him. He didn't like having her look through him. He wanted her looking at him.

But Mona still stood in the way. Every time he looked at Fancy, Mona's shadow was right there at her shoulder.

"Ready to go?" Paul came in the back door like he always did, in midconversation.

Fancy and Mrs. Sartin, who had asked Fancy to call her Miriam, were washing tomatoes for canning.

"Anything more I can do here?" Fancy asked Miriam.

"Not a thing. You two just go along."

"We'll be back early this afternoon," Fancy promised. Paul had to be at work by four but he'd wanted to take her to Eureka Springs again.

She'd accepted the invitation eagerly. The tension between her and Rader had grown steadily since Brian had left two days earlier. It seemed the more they wanted to avoid each other, the more they ran into each other. And every time Fancy saw him, there was suspicion in his face. Even a few hours break would help.

"You two have fun," Miriam said, ruffling her son's hair.

Paul kissed his mother's cheek, then swatted playfully at her. Fancy watched them jealously. Theirs was the kind of relationship she'd have wanted with Mona, if there had ever been a hope for it.

Fancy followed Paul out to the motorcycle and climbed on behind him. When they roared down the drive, she felt free. During the past three weeks, they'd made several trips to Eureka Springs. While Paul worked, Fancy wandered through the shops but invariably ended up at the park listening to the musicians.

To her surprise, the guitarists began handing her their instruments to fill in while they took a break. She'd overcome her reluctance after the first time or two and played, loving the feel of the music flowing from her fingers, wishing she had her own instrument again.

She became a regular with the group, playing with the guys two or three times a week. They developed a playful rapport that she cherished. They were taciturn, crusty, but she also noticed they were careful to teach her the tunes that were a large part of their lives.

She laughed and joked with them as they played, enjoying the appreciation of their audience. Sometimes Charlie would jump up and pull Fancy to her feet to execute an intricate two-step dance. The crowds grew, clapping and laughing their appreciation. Their

concerts became an almost daily event with people
bringing their lawn chairs and spending the afternoon
drinking lemonade and chatting quietly while enjoying the music. Fancy loved it. She'd never felt so alive,
so carefree, as during those afternoons, and her love
of music was obvious to everyone who saw her per-
form.

As Fancy rode behind Paul, the wind in her face,
she looked forward to seeing Charlie and Ben and the
others. It was a perfect summer day. The morning was
so bright, it almost glowed, but by noon the temperature would reach ninety.

Before long, she would be going back to San Francisco, whether she had anything from Mona's estate or
not. She had to begin thinking about getting on with
her life—with or without Rader Malone.

Paul parked the cycle in front of a quaint little store
with a faded and peeling sign over it that might have
read Fred's Emporium.

"What a cute little shop," Fancy enthused.

"Fred's quite a fellow," Paul said, opening the door
for her.

A small bell over the door tinkled, announcing their
arrival. The shop smelled a little musty, and the old
signs, glass pieces, old toys and books were dusty.
Fancy was enchanted.

"People in San Francisco would give an arm and a
leg for some of these things. They're into art deco, you
know. Stuff from the fifties."

"They should see Fred's attic," Paul said, laughing.

"Paul," a wizened old man called as he came from the back room through a garishly patterned curtain.

"Fred, I'd like you to meet Fancy Connors."

"Oh, your musician friend." Fred smiled and took her hand in both of his. "I've heard about you from Charlie. He's very impressed with your talent."

Fancy flushed with pride. "I enjoy playing with them. They're very kind."

"I think you have something for me," Paul reminded Fred.

"It's right here." Fred bent to reach under the counter.

Fred's efforts brought forth a flat-top guitar that he handed to Paul. Fancy blinked, not certain what was happening when Paul started to hand the instrument to her.

"It's not new and it's not 'fancy', but it's a guitar."

She looked at the instrument. It certainly wasn't new, but it had been lovingly cared for. "It's very nice, but—"

"It's yours."

She was stunned. "You can't mean that. I—I don't have the money—"

"It's a gift."

"I can't accept a gift like this."

"Yes, you can. I won't take no for an answer," Paul insisted, shoving the guitar into her hands.

"But . . ."

"You love to play and you don't have a guitar. Besides, Charlie, Ben and the others would never forgive me if I took it back."

"They know about this?"

Paul grinned. "Who do you think knew it was here?"

Fancy blinked back tears of gratitude. The gift was such a warm, loving, unselfish gesture, and there had been too few of those in her life.

"They're hoping you'll sit in with them again. Teach them a few of those fancy strokes."

She swallowed the lump in her throat and hugged the guitar to her chest. "Thank you, Paul. Thank you, Fred. No one's ever done anything like this for me before."

Paul hugged her with open affection. "Then let's go see if the guys are in the park."

They mounted the cycle again, with Fancy balancing the guitar on her hip. When they arrived at the park, Charlie and Ben were on the platform, picking simple tunes. When they saw Fancy and Paul, they waved them over. Fancy ran toward them, the guitar lifted over her head in a joyous salute.

"I see you got 'er," Charlie growled.

"Thank you," Fancy said, smiling, hugging them with abandon. She'd had few close friends in her life and cherished them greatly and affectionately. "I noticed it has new strings. You thought of everything." She stroked the wood lovingly, and her fingers drifted over the strings as if she caressed them.

"Can't have a string breakin' in the middle of somethin'," Ben muttered, his thumb testing a string on his own instrument.

Fancy smiled to herself. The crusty old musicians didn't want a lot of recognition for their gift but they were pleased at her response. In return, she would play her best.

Chapter Seven

It was nearly dark when Paul dropped Fancy off at the back door of the house. Miriam had long since left but there was a note from her on the kitchen table. She'd left steaks in the refrigerator in marinade, fresh corn-on-the-cob ready to cook and tomatoes for slicing. Sharon, it said, was coming for dinner.

Fancy crumpled the note and started upstairs to shower. She met Rader coming down.

"Fancy."

"Hello, Rader." How ridiculously formal we are, she thought. It was sad that it had come down to this.

"What's that?"

Fancy brought the guitar out from behind her.

"Where'd you get it?"

The set of his face made Fancy's nerves tighten. "It was a gift. From friends."

Anger flashed through him. How like Mona that sounded. The woman had made a living on gifts from "friends."

"From whom?" he demanded coldly.

Stung, Fancy lifted her chin in defense. She stood two steps below him, which put her at a disadvantage.

"Paul and others."

She'd worked fast, damn her, Rader thought. Making conquests within weeks of her arrival in the somewhat desolate area couldn't have been easy, but she'd done it.

"Give it back."

"What?" Fancy could hardly believe her ears.

"Give it back."

She met his gaze and made up her mind in that moment. "No. I'm not giving it back. It was a gift and I treasure it. To return it would be an insult to them."

There was nothing more he could say or do. She was, after all, an adult. If she chose to live on the generosity of others, then there was nothing he could do. Except tell her to leave. And he couldn't do that, yet.

Reluctantly, he went on down the stairs, more determined than ever to find out what made Fancy Connors tick. Then he could get her out of his mind forever.

After she'd changed into clean jeans and an oxford shirt, Fancy returned to the kitchen to lay out the steaks to warm to room temperature and start water for the corn. The doorbell rang, and she heard Rader answer it. She hurried to finish her preparations, hoping to avoid Rader and Sharon. Miriam's note had said Rader intended to eat on the patio, and she'd set the table out there. Brushing her hands together and glancing around the kitchen, Fancy was satisfied everything was ready.

"What are you doing in here?" Rader asked.

"Getting dinner ready. I won't be in your way," she returned, pulling off the apron she **wore**. She wasn't looking for another confrontation.

"That's not what I meant...."

"I'm sure you and Sharon want to be alone," Fancy interrupted.

Rader's eyes narrowed. "Like you and Paul?"

"Somewhat different, I think."

"You and Paul seem to be seeing a lot of one another."

"We're friends. He's good enough to drive me back and forth to Eureka."

"What's your relationship?"

Fancy stopped halfway to the door. "What do you mean?"

"What's going on between you and Paul?"

Resentment flared. "Nothing. We're friends."

"You're spending a lot of time together. You often don't get home until late."

"I think that's my business."

"It's mine when it's Paul."

"Why? His own mother isn't concerned."

"This is my house. What goes on here is my concern."

"What do you think we're doing?"

Rader didn't know what to say. How could he tell her his imagination had driven him crazy for days. That he'd imagined Fancy and Paul together, touching, kissing, loving. How could he say to her, "Be here. Stay here." He couldn't. Not when he had no idea why she was really here at all.

Fancy pushed on the door. "I know what you think and you're wrong," she said. "The corn is ready to go into the water, and the steaks are ready for the grill." She went through the door, nodded to Sharon, who waited in the living room, and ran upstairs.

In her room, Fancy threw herself on the bed and picked up the guitar. She gently plucked the strings, remembering her dreams, trying to tell herself to let them go. But she couldn't. Not yet.

About eight, Fancy returned downstairs. Sharon was just coming out of the kitchen. "Oh, there you are. I just left the things on the cabinet. Hope that's all right."

Fancy went in and stared at the mess Sharon had left. The dirty grill was in the sink, the plates stacked beside it. The dessert plates, knives, forks and glasses were strung down the counter.

Letting the door swing shut behind her, Fancy tied on the apron. She couldn't leave this mess for Miriam. She rinsed the dishes and put them in the dishwasher, then ran hot sudsy water for the grill. Plunging her hands into the water, she began scrubbing the grill with a wire scratcher.

"Why didn't you just leave that for Mother?" Sharon said as she walked to the refrigerator for ice.

"She has enough to do," Fancy said, concentrating on the grill.

"That's her job."

Fancy ignored her.

"When is your little vacation over?" Sharon asked, leaning against the cabinet, sipping a fresh glass of iced tea.

"I'm not sure."

"Rader is a very busy man."

"I'm aware of that."

"You're breaking his concentration."

Fancy doubted that. Rader was always a very focused man. "Am I? Why are you so worried about that?"

Sharon sipped her tea. "Rader and I have many things in common."

"And that means...?" Fancy knew what it meant, but wanted Sharon to clarify her relationship with Rader. So far she'd received mixed signals.

"I'm just interested in protecting him. Making certain he can work."

"I thought you were in banking, not baby-sitting."

Sharon's eyebrow lifted in recognition of Fancy's barb, but just then Rader strode in. His glance went from one woman to the other, sensing the tension in the room.

"What's going on here?"

"Oh, nothing, darling," Sharon said, linking her arm with his. "I was just telling Fancy she didn't have to clean up our mess."

"That's right. We were going to do that."

Fancy's glance flicked from Rader to Sharon. "Well, it's finished now." She rinsed the grill and dried it, ignoring them both.

"Rader, we have some other things to discuss," Sharon reminded him.

"You go ahead. I've looked at the prospectus, and Brian has read it. I have his opinion. I'll be there in a minute."

So, Fancy thought with satisfaction, perhaps Sharon's attempt to present a picture of intimacy between herself and Rader was nothing more than a business meeting. Interesting. No wonder she was a little paranoid, considering she'd had her eye on Rader for years.

When the door swung shut behind Sharon, Rader placed his hand on Fancy's arm and turned her around.

"What was going on when I walked in?"

"Sharon told you."

His dark eyes met hers. "I don't understand you, Fancy."

"What's to understand?"

"Why are you here?"

"I thought we settled that before. I wanted to see the house, see you."

"Yet you get away from here whenever you can. You've spent more time with Paul in Eureka Springs than you have here."

Fancy shrugged. "I've met some very nice, very interesting people in Eureka Springs. You're working, so I go there."

Rader didn't believe her. She saw it in his eyes and in the jump of the muscle in his jaw.

"Now, if there's nothing else, I'm tired. Sharon's waiting for you."

"Brian is coming tomorrow," Rader announced.

Fancy waited for the rest, knowing Rader was studying her intently for some reaction.

"He should arrive around noon. We have some things to go over, then he wants to talk to you."

"That's fine."

"I thought perhaps you and Paul had a date."

Fancy drew a deep breath of resignation. "Rader, Paul is a friend. Nothing more. I'd have thought you'd be pleased not to have me underfoot. I seem to... irritate you for some reason. Would you rather I left?"

"No. I invited you here for the summer."

Well, she'd asked, but he hadn't given her the answer she wanted. She wanted Rader to say he wanted her to stay, not because he felt obligated but because he really wanted her there. But that seemed a vain hope. So, she'd stay until the estate was settled, then return to San Francisco and the life she'd begun to build before everything had fallen apart.

"Thank you," she said, and tried to move past him.

Rader blocked her path. "I don't want your thanks."

She looked up at him and swallowed dryly. When he was this close, she couldn't ignore how attractive he was and how much hope she'd pinned on this trip.

"Then what do you want?" she breathed, not trusting her voice.

The more
you love romance . . .
the more
you'll love this offer

FREE!

Mail this heart today! (See inside)

**Join us on a Silhouette® Honeymoon
and we'll give you
4 free books
A free Victorian picture frame
And a free mystery gift**

IT'S A
SILHOUETTE HONEYMOON—
A SWEETHEART OF A FREE OFFER!
HERE'S WHAT YOU GET:

1. **Four New Silhouette Romance™ Novels—FREE!**
Take a Silhouette Honeymoon with your four exciting romances—yours FREE from Silhouette Reader Service™. Each of these hot-off-the-press novels brings you the passion and tenderness of today's greatest love stories . . . your free passports to bright new worlds of love and foreign adventure.

2. **Lovely Victorian Picture Frame—FREE!**

This lovely Victorian pewter-finish miniature is perfect for displaying a treasured photograph. And it's yours FREE as added thanks for giving our Reader Service a try!

3. **An Exciting Mystery Bonus—FREE!**
You'll be thrilled with this surprise gift. It is useful as well as practical.

4. **Free Home Delivery!**
Join the Silhouette Reader Service™ and enjoy the convenience of pre-viewing 6 new books every month delivered right to your home. Each book is yours for only $2.25* each. And there is no extra charge for postage and handling. It's a sweetheart of a deal for you! If you're not completely satisfied, you may cancel at anytime, for any reason, simply by sending us a note or shipping statement marked "cancel" or by re-turning any shipment to us at our cost.

5. **Free Insiders' Newsletter!**
You'll get our monthly newsletter, packed with news about your favorite writers, upcoming books, even recipes from your favorite authors.

6. **More Surprise Gifts!**
Because our home subscribers are our most valued readers, when you join the Silhouette Reader Service™, we'll be sending you additional free gifts from time to time—as a token of our appreciation.

START YOUR SILHOUETTE HONEYMOON TODAY—JUST COM-PLETE, DETACH AND MAIL YOUR FREE-OFFER CARD

*Terms and prices subject to change without notice. Sales tax applicable in NY.

START YOUR
SILHOUETTE HONEYMOON TODAY.
JUST COMPLETE, DETACH AND MAIL YOUR
FREE-OFFER CARD.

If offer card below is missing write to:
Silhouette Reader Service, 3010 Walden Ave.,
P.O. Box 1867, Buffalo, NY 14269-1867.

DETACH AND MAIL TODAY.

BUSINESS REPLY MAIL
FIRST CLASS MAIL   PERMIT NO. 717   BUFFALO, NY

POSTAGE WILL BE PAID BY ADDRESSEE

SILHOUETTE READER SERVICE
3010 WALDEN AVE
PO BOX 1867
BUFFALO NY 14240-9952

NO POSTAGE
NECESSARY
IF MAILED
IN THE
UNITED STATES

Rader studied her face, noting that some of the paleness had been replaced by a light tan. She looked healthier, less tired. She was still very thin and sometimes she rested a hand against her stomach as though she felt nauseated or something. What could be wrong? She wasn't about to tell him. Maybe he'd have more information about her tomorrow when Brian arrived.

His gaze fell to her mouth, which was parted moistly. Her throat moved as she swallowed again. Her hair was slipping loose from the braid that lay over her shoulder, the rubber-band fastening resting on her breast.

"Maybe this." He touched her braid, his finger sliding down the silken plait. It was as if he touched her skin, her breast. Her stomach tightened with desire so intense she knew he must have sensed it.

Her breath caught, drawing his attention back to her mouth. Suddenly he knew what he wanted and his gaze flicked to her eyes, which widened with awareness. God, she was a witch. Bewitching.

"I'm not here for your entertainment," she whispered.

"I didn't ask you to be."

"Then what am I here for?" If she kept asking, maybe one day she'd get the right answer.

"Curiosity."

"Yours or mine?"

"For right now, mine."

Fancy watched the change come over his face. When his head bent toward her, she waited with anticipation, her eyes drifting closed as his lips brushed hers.

When his mouth closed over hers, all thought fled. She only felt his lips and she breathed in the fragrance of his cologne. Her hand rested on his upper arm for balance. And when his lips coaxed hers apart, she clung to him, moving into his arms without full comprehension of what was happening. She responded blindly.

It was a dream. A dream she'd cherished for years. And its reality was as sweet as she'd hoped. When his tongue teased hers, she opened to him, and when his arms pulled her against him, she went willingly. This was the dream.

Rader leaned back against the cabinet, drawing Fancy between his spread legs. Her arms went around his waist and she rested fully against him. She was sweet. Every bit as sweet as he'd anticipated. It was then that he realized he wanted more, realized where they were.

When the kiss ended, reality came like a flash of cold water. Fancy pushed abruptly out of Rader's arms.

"Sharon's waiting for you."

Straightening, Rader caught her again. "Is that what you came for?"

She granted him only a glance before striding quickly from the kitchen. Hoping he wouldn't follow, Fancy ran up the stairs and to her room. There, in the darkness, she leaned against the door and touched her lips gently with trembling fingertips. Just when she'd convinced herself she should leave, that there was no hope for her and Rader, he did something like this.

Maybe, just maybe, she should stay. After all, Brian was coming tomorrow. Perhaps he had some good news for her.

"Hello, Brian," Fancy greeted the attorney at the door.

"Whew! It's hot!" He dragged his tie loose as he stepped inside.

"Then I'll get you something cool to drink," she promised. "How was your flight?"

"A two-hour delay in St. Louis, but other than that, just fine. It gave me an opportunity to catch up on some paperwork."

"Go on into the den and make yourself comfortable. I'll bring your drink. Rader will be down in a minute."

Fancy returned a few minutes later with three glasses of tea.

"I have some more mail for you, Fancy. Another one of those letters from a hospital in San Francisco. Are you sure it's not something I should handle?"

"I'm sure," Fancy said, taking the envelope and accepting the magazines and flyers he handed her. If she gave Brian the past-due bill, Rader would know how desperately she needed money and make the wrong assumptions.

"Then what is it?" Rader asked as he entered the room.

"Nothing. Here's your tea."

Rader accepted the glass and sat across from Fancy. "More fashion magazines?"

"Yes, and just in time, too," she said, knowing that was what Rader expected to hear.

"I have something else here for you," Brian handed Fancy another envelope.

She opened it slowly and stared at the check inside.

"It isn't much. Only five hundred dollars. But I felt you deserved something from the estate."

"Why, thank you. I'm surprised."

"It looks like we may be making some progress. The preliminary FAA report is in and there's nothing suspect. And all the bills are in and being processed. There won't be much left. Perhaps a couple of thousand. But—" he shrugged "—I guess that's better than nothing, considering Mona didn't have the foresight to have an insurance policy."

She once had one, Fancy remembered. But they couldn't keep up the payments on it, and Fancy had had to let it lapse the year before Mona became ill.

Clutching the envelope, Fancy stood. "If there's nothing else . . ."

"That's it. As soon as everything is settled, I'll give you a call."

With a nod to Rader, Fancy left the den and went upstairs. Inside her room, she looked at the check again. Money. Now she could begin paying some of her own bills. And there was the prescription that needed refilling.

Tomorrow, when they went to Eureka Springs, she could get the check cashed and have the prescription moved to the small pharmacy where she stopped for a fountain soda. She whirled around in joy. It was surprising how a little money could change one's attitude about life in general. Perhaps she understood a little of how Mona felt. But she had to save as much as she could. Brian had said there wouldn't be much coming from the estate. Every dollar counted if she was to start all over again.

Over Paul's protest, Fancy insisted on contributing to the gas he used transporting her back and forth to Eureka Springs. Slowly, she began to put her life in a pattern. She rose at seven, after Rader was already at work in his first-floor office, ate breakfast and visited with Miriam. Then, if Rader planned on being home that evening, Fancy received instructions on preparing dinner.

During the rare days that she didn't go to Eureka Springs, Fancy helped Miriam with canning vegetables or some other chore. A strong rapport grew between the women, and Rader often found them sitting at the table with pans of green beans or some other vegetable in their laps, laughing together. And that's the way he found them this morning.

The first time Miriam saw Rader's scowl, she attributed it to a writing problem, and Fancy let her believe that. But soon, even Miriam noticed Rader's continuing bad mood.

"What's the matter with that boy? Anybody'd think he needed a dose of castor oil," Miriam grumbled after Rader had stomped out with a fresh mug of coffee.

Fancy suppressed a giggle at the idea of anyone giving Rader Malone a spoon of the vile tasting oily medicine that seemed to be the mainstay of the Ozark Hills people.

"I think I'm what's bothering him," Fancy admitted. "My being here."

"Aw," Miriam dismissed. "He wants you here or he wouldn't have asked you to come. Rader Malone doesn't do anything he doesn't want to."

"I don't know," Fancy said. "He's so sure I'm like Mona that he's probably regretting the invitation. He hated her so."

"Ah, yes. Mona. The butterfly."

"Did you know her?"

"No. No one in the valley knew Mona. She was too busy."

Fancy knew how "busy" Mona was. Busy meant caring for her own interests. Busy meant shopping, talking on the phone, taking vacations. Busy meant filling every hour, every minute, with something, anything.

That afternoon Fancy went to the Sartin house to help Miriam make tomato preserves. When she'd first heard of it, Fancy wrinkled her nose. Miriam had laughed and invited her to watch the process and taste the results.

"Bring that guitar, too," Miriam had said. "Paul talks so much about your playing, I want to hear you."

Pleased, Fancy and her guitar rode over to the old farm house just after noon. By two o'clock, she was elbow deep in skinned tomatoes. By three o'clock, she knew about making tomato preserves and stood over a hot stove stirring a mixture of tomatoes, lemon and orange slices and spices. She was still apprehensive about how it would taste.

By five o'clock, rows of preserves sat on the cabinet in shiny pint jars. Fancy relaxed at the kitchen table, idly plucking at the guitar strings and sipping iced tea while Miriam prepared to fry chicken and make biscuits.

Paul came in a short time later and sat down at the table to tell about his day and tease Miriam and Fancy. He took Fancy on a tour of the farm, showing her the flourishing garden, the glowing beds of flowers. Fancy laughed delightedly at Paul's funny descriptions of things he'd tried and failed.

Over dinner, Fancy felt herself relax for the first time in weeks. Perhaps for the first time in years. After dinner, they went out on the big front porch with slices of homemade apple pie topped with ice cream to watch the sun set.

"Play Mom a tune," Paul coaxed. "Play that one Charlie showed you yesterday."

Fancy picked up her guitar and began to strum. Soon she became lost in the music, moving from one tune to another, sitting with her eyes closed, her fingers moving on the strings.

Occasionally she hummed along or gently sang the words. Then, realizing she was growing too melancholy, she stopped a moment, her palm on the strings to still the chord.

Suddenly, she broke into "Rocky Top," then "Foggy Mountain Breakdown," followed by others with a quick, invigorating beat. Miriam and Paul were clapping, tapping toes and laughing when a car pulled into the drive, flashing them with the headlights.

Sharon got out and came up the walk as Fancy finished a rousing solo version of "Dueling Banjos."

"My, I wasn't aware you were so talented," Sharon commented.

"Fancy is *very* good," Paul emphasized.

"Best I've ever heard," Miriam enthused, "and I've heard some of the best."

"Why aren't you performing? Make a career of music...back in San Francisco."

Fancy got the message. "I have," she admitted.

"Oh? I wasn't aware of that."

Paul jumped in, apparently sensing Fancy's discomfort. "She's been playing with some of the musicians in Eureka Springs."

"How interesting," Sharon commented without much interest. "Well, I have a date and I'm running a little late...."

Sharon hurried inside and Fancy concentrated on plucking out a small tune. She knew who Sharon was seeing and it hurt. Maybe she should just give up and get a bus ticket back to San Francisco.

Thunder rumbled in the distance, and Fancy looked up to see lightning playing on the horizon. A breeze had sprung up and the temperature was noticeably cooler.

"We're in for a summer storm," Miriam commented.

"I'd better get back...home, if someone can give me ride."

Paul jumped up and executed a mockingly low bow. "The open chariot is at your disposal, madam."

"Thank you, sir," Fancy said with a deep curtsy.

There was a light in the living room when Paul parked the cycle and walked Fancy to the door of Rader's house, but Fancy knew no one was at home. She fished a key Miriam had given her out of her jeans pocket and unlocked the door.

"Thanks, Paul. Thanks for all the rides and this," she said, lifting the guitar. "Everything."

"You're welcome," he said. "Payment made in full with a tune."

Fancy stood in the door and watched until the cycle's taillights disappeared. She enjoyed being with Paul and with his mother. Too bad Rader didn't understand that she had no ulterior motives in counting them as friends.

Fancy went upstairs to her room. She sat at the window and watched the storm sweep across the valley. The rain came down in torrents for over an hour. The thunder crashed and rumbled while lightning forked crazily. The lights flickered again and again.

Finally she took a shower, but she wasn't sleepy. Maybe it was the storm or maybe knowing Rader was out with Sharon that wouldn't let her sleep. She decided to go down and light a fire in the fireplace. Perhaps play a little.

Not having a robe, Fancy decided to look for something comfortable to wear in Rader's room. With a towel around her, she went to his room and opened the closet. There wasn't a robe, but toward the back was an old oxford shirt. It was much too large for her, but it would be loose and comfortable. Hoping Rader wouldn't miss it, Fancy slipped it on and turned back the cuffs. Carrying her guitar, she went downstairs to the den.

The storm had brought with it a damp chill, and Fancy lit the fire laid on the hearth. It caught quickly and she stared into the flames. Where are you, Rader? I wish you were here . . . with me.

Chapter Eight

Lost in thought, Fancy's fingers moved lovingly over the guitar. She sat on the rug in front of the fire, her legs crossed Indian fashion to support the guitar on one knee. Her hair hung loose over her shoulders, one side tucked behind her ear to control it, the other hanging in a curtain to shimmer in the light of the flickering fire.

The storm crashed about the house as Rader stepped inside the front door. Shaking the rain from his jacket, he tossed it over the newel post to dry. The house was quiet. At first he thought he was alone, then he heard the low strumming sounds of a guitar and followed them.

He stopped in the doorway, absorbing the primitive look of her. She was a wood nymph sitting so unselfconsciously before his fire. The shirt, which he recognized as his own, hung loosely on her slim frame, accentuating a certain vulnerability that was seldom evident.

A wealth of golden hair brushed the floor with its length, and he felt a sudden urge to bury his hands in it. With the firelight behind her, she was a silhouette. He saw the swell of her breast, the rounded hip, through the thin cloth of the loose shirt.

Her long legs were encased in jeans so worn they were skin soft, her thighs rounded and firm. Her skin was touched golden by the fire. Her fingers moved over the strings of the guitar in a sensual caress that made him remember their touch. He remembered, too, the pads of callouses that he'd discovered that first night and now knew the reason for them. Why had she not told him she played then?

He recognized the tune she played softly as ''Greensleeves.'' Her low contralto voice hummed the tune before softly breathing the melancholy words. Her face was shadowed, but her high cheek bones stood out in relief. He knew her eyes would be golden, half-shuttered, as she lost herself completely in her music and whatever else occupied her mind. Rader wished he could read her thoughts at this moment. Who were they of?

Fancy was alerted to his presence by a slight sound in the doorway. She looked up, startled, her eyes wide with surprise. Her lips parted as if she would speak, but he interrupted.

''Go on. I'd like to hear you play.''

Fancy rested the guitar in her lap. ''I'm finished.'' She glance at him again, seeing the rain glistening in his dark hair. "I thought you were out for the evening."

He was disappointed she had stopped playing and knew he was the reason.

"There were flash-flood warnings so I took Sharon home before the roads became dangerous."

The mention of Sharon's name took away some of the warmth of the room. "I see. Well, I'll go upstairs."

Rader had moved closer, becoming a part of the shadows. The firelight flickered across his face, and she was caught watching it move over the strong planes of his features. He surprised her by sitting at the edge of the rug, just out of reach. His dark eyes were intent upon her. His closeness unnerved her further.

"I'd like to hear you play."

The second request was softly spoken and a tingle moved across her taut nerves.

Fancy studied him for a moment, measuring the sincerity of his request. Finally she picked up the guitar and let her fingers move gently across the strings. She fell into more modern tunes. "The Rose," a Bette Midler song she particularly liked, began to evolve from her random plucking. Then she moved into the more familiar country tunes of "The Green Green Grass of Home" and "Scarlet Ribbons." Rader picked up on her mood immediately.

"You're a difficult woman to understand, Fancy. Your moods are mercurial. I suppose that is your musician's temperament. But when you play, it's like a transformation takes place. You become the music.

It's a gauge of your happiness or sadness, your lone-liness. I've noticed in other people that that sort of thing occurs when one has little else into which to pour themselves."

Fancy ignored his invitation to comment on his perceptions and continued to concentrate on the gui-tar.

"You're melancholy tonight. Is it the storm? Or are you just unhappy?"

Surprised by the question and disturbed by his as-tuteness, Fancy hesitated before answering. "I sup-pose it's the storm." She continued playing, watching the strings as her fingers moved upon them to avoid looking at Rader.

"I watched the rain coming, moving across the val-ley. I could smell it, smell the freshness of it, feel it on my face before it really arrived. I've never done that before. It was a marvelous feeling."

She strummed a few more cords. Rader sat and lis-tened.

"Even the thunder and lightning are different here. Closer. Much more real. Exciting in a way. I felt...alive. More vividly alive than ever before." She glanced up at him, a little embarrassed. "It's hard to explain. I found a part of me I hadn't known was there."

Rader watched her fiddle with the guitar a mo-ment. "That's how I feel about this place. It's like...recharging your batteries. After a trip to the city, I can come back here and relax, find a peace that exists nowhere else on earth."

They spoke in hushed tones as if afraid they might shatter the fragile truce between them.

"I can understand that. I'm going to miss it...." She stopped, reluctant to introduce a subject that was so volatile.

"When you go back to San Francisco? But that won't be for a while yet. You have the summer." He smiled. "You might change your mind. Summer here is hot, dry and dusty. By the time fall arrives, we're more than ready for the cool air and rains. Remember? Sometimes the heat lays in the valley like a blanket, smothering until you think you can't breathe. But the rains are like a spiritual revival."

A smile curved her lips. She had forgotten. "San Francisco offers a different kind of summer—the big-city kind, with heat, tourists, frayed tempers and hot cement. But there's an excitement about the city that stays in the blood. You stay in spite of the drawbacks."

"And you?"

"I stay because... because it's all I know."

Rader studied her a long moment. "I would have thought you'd strike out for greener, bigger pastures. You're a beautiful young woman. Talented. I'm sure there have been opportunities... New York, Los Angeles. Places where you could make a name for yourself."

Fancy shrugged her shoulders lightly, causing the half-buttoned shirt to fall open. The first swell of her breasts caught his breath. His stomach tightened in reaction to her very basic and uncontrived sensuality.

It was as if she didn't realize the potency of her womanly body. She sat there as guileless as a child, totally unconscious of the effect of her near nudity upon him. In the overly-large shirt with the first shadows of cleavage, she seemed both waif and woman. Her sexuality plucked at all his senses.

"Making a name never appealed to me. Nor did traveling."

He pushed down fast-growing responses to her with sarcasm. "No? You did quite a lot of it when you were younger."

They were approaching sensitive subjects, subjects that invariably sparked arguments. Fancy sought to evade them by retreat. "I'm going upstairs."

But as she rolled to her knees, Rader quickly moved in front of her. "I'm sorry. I shouldn't have said that. I seem to always be saying the wrong things to you. Please. Stay for a while."

He knelt in front of her within touching distance. She was too aware of him, too aware of his dark gaze moving over her. Before she thought, her tongue slipped out to dampen her lips in a nervous gesture, that, she recognized too late, could be called inviting. Rader accepted the invitation by leaning forward and brushing her lips with his own.

Fancy swayed on her knees, reaching out a hand to balance herself. He caught her long fingers against his chest. She felt the heat emanating from him and it drew her. Again he tasted her lips, but then returned to capture her mouth.

His tongue traced the outline of her lips, investigating the soft inner side of them. She returned the kiss, darting her tongue past his to taste and tantalize. With a groan, he caught her to him, crushing her slim form into his before carrying her with him to the floor.

The rug was soft at her back as he pressed her into it. His mouth became a torment—tasting, nipping, tantalizing, as he was caught in the fervor of the storm being loosed within them both.

As the thunder crashed outside, her heart thundered inside her chest. Rader measured its cadence with his thumb as he caressed the soft line of her throat while his mouth tasted the dewy softness of her skin.

Unable to resist his sensual teasing, Fancy buried her fingers in his dark hair and drew his attention back to her mouth. She'd wanted him for so long, dreamed of this so long, she forgot all the reasons it shouldn't happen. None of the reasons mattered.

She took the initiative, molding her lips to his and demanding to share the intimacy of his mouth. She hardly knew when the buttons of her shirt parted, but the warmth of his hand on her stomach made her arch mindlessly against him with a low groan of desire.

Her fingers fumbled with the buttons of his dark shirt, finally pulling the fabric loose from his belt to allow her hands access. When she explored freely, her fingers floating over the hard contours of his chest and stomach, searching out the flat male nipples, the groan was his.

Rader's mouth caught hers again in a driving passion that erased all logical thought from her mind. Only blind reaction remained and her body raged with the need to experience all of him.

Matching her frustration, Rader quickly jerked off his own shirt then slipped the shirt from her back. His dark gaze fell over her slim, pale form and she felt as well as heard his breath catch.

"You're exquisite," he breathed. His hand ran down the length of her as if to memorize everything. His thumb expertly slipped free the button of her jeans and pulled open the zipper. "I tried to imagine what you would be like, what your body would look like. But I wasn't even close."

He cupped her breast, molding it, brushing the nipple with his thumb. Her fingers dug into his shoulder. Her legs shifted restlessly as he continued to tease her.

She begged him with her body to allow her the same freedom he enjoyed. Her hand followed the soft mat of hair across his chest to where it disappeared beneath his belt.

Arching hungrily into him, she reveled in the feel of him against her. Her breasts felt full and aching as they pressed into the rough contours of his chest. Her legs slid tantalizingly against the muscle-hardened thighs and sinewy calves, and her hips rocked into his in silent petition. The worn jeans molding his body were like a layer of skin.

With a smothered groan, Rader gathered her close to him before laying her back across his arm to allow himself full view of her. Her amber eyes were slitted, watching his taut face. The flesh was tight across his cheeks and his eyes were black with desire. Her gaze measured his body, appreciating its symmetry and the differences that made the male and female complement each other.

Her hand rested on his side in the hollow created just above his hip. Her thumb measured the bone of his hip, moving into the soft flesh of his belly. His caught breath of response brought a smile to her mobile lips.

"You like that, don't you? You like to know you turn me on, that when I see you, I want you." His voice was a husky whisper caressing her heightened senses. "We've been circling one another for weeks. That's why we argue, you know. Because it's a way of releasing the tension."

His mouth caught hers again in an aggression that fired her own. Her fingers kneaded his flesh, following the contours of his body in a sensuous search. This was crazy, being here with Rader. She knew it would only make things more difficult. But for this moment, it was right.

Her long fingers clasped the curve of his hip to draw him nearer. The storm was no longer outside. It was inside her, raging and demanding, the thunder and lightning a part of them.

Rader moved over her, his relentless passion driving, demanding. Fancy moved with him, opening to him, inviting him. "I need you, Fancy," his rough voice whispered in her ear as she arched to him, his warm breath fanning her skin. "I need you now, tonight. It doesn't matter who else you've been with, what you've been...."

His words smashed into her brain, paralyzing all her senses. Fancy stiffened in his arms. Tears stung her eyes. Nothing had changed. No matter what he said, Rader still believed she was a second Mona.

"Let me go, Rader." Fancy pushed against him ineffectually, turning her face away from the accusation she knew was there.

"Fancy?" He didn't understand the sudden change in her.

"Let me go." She pushed at him again, struggling to get out of his arms.

Suddenly his fingers bit into her shoulders. "What is this? Another trick? Some kind of come-on?" His voice lowered menacingly. "Another of Mona's well-learned ploys? What do you want? What payment will be enough?"

"Just let me go, Rader." This time her voice was normal. Her nerves were more calm as anger replaced passion in full force.

His lips curled back from his teeth, and his whispered words were like spears in the flesh of her heart. "You're playing a dangerous game, Fancy. Didn't your mother tell you not to play with a man's libido? Didn't she include timing in her lessons?"

His voice was menacingly husky, growling the hurtful words. His fingers caught her chin to bring her face around. She kept her eyes tightly closed to avoid looking into the angry fire dancing in his eyes. A cold stone lay heavily in her stomach, and her nerves were so taut she quivered inside.

Her heart was breaking. What had made her believe things could ever be different between herself and Rader?

"What else did Mona teach you, Fancy?" His voice became caressing.

He moved against her suggestively, and in spite of her resolve, her body responded. "Rader..."

Rader heard the apprehension in her voice and realized what he was doing and where they were.

She could almost feel the anger melt away from him and she waited apprehensively for what he would do next.

"Fancy, I don't know what to do with you. I don't know what to give you, how to deal with what I'm feeling."

She was surprised. Expecting recriminations, his candid revelation that he was uncertain about what was between them threw her even more off balance.

"You seemed to have no problem with that before. You're a very self-confident man."

His short laugh was self-mocking. "I wish it was that simple. Physically, you're the most provocative woman I've ever known." He rested on his elbows over her, his body warm against hers. "I tried to imagine what you looked like all grown up, but I wasn't even close to imagining your natural sexuality, the loveliness of your body, the freshness of your spirit. But there's more to it than that. I have an idea of you that doesn't match what I see and feel. Right now, I don't understand any of it."

Her white teeth nibbled at her lower lip, catching his attention and drawing his thumb to trace its outline.

"Do you have to understand it? Can't you just accept... today? Accept me just as I am?" If she could have him just for today, maybe that would be enough.

His hand caught her about the neck, his fingers a gentle noose. "No. I can't. I have to know you inside and out. I have to know exactly what you are. Who you are. I can't afford not to be sure."

"Why? Why is it so important?"

"Because I'm not Kurt. Because I learned from his mistakes."

She listened, unable to breathe, unable to think.

"Kurt loved my mother. Loved her deeply. When she died, he was devastated. For a long time, he wasn't seriously interested in anyone."

Rader drew in a deep breath, then continued. "Then he met Mona. He was captivated by her, blinded by her beauty, drawn by her ability to make him feel like a man. She made him feel alive again. He didn't recognize it was all a game to Mona. A savage game meant to further her own interests. The interest of money and how to spend it. I know firsthand."

A coldness began to creep through Fancy's body. She knew the truth, but she didn't want to hear it now. Especially not now. "Please... please, Rader. Don't... don't say these things."

She knew what was coming and didn't want to hear it. The incident had stood between them for years. Perhaps it was best left alone after all.

Rader shifted, making his own body leap again in awareness of her femaleness. But he controlled his desire and continued.

"When Mona came to my room that night, I knew for certain what kind of woman she was. She was looking for a younger man than Kurt. Oh, she knew all the tricks, believe me. When I turned her down, she was angry and threatened to tell Kurt I seduced her if I said anything. As it happens, it came out anyway. But what she told him was a lie.

"I could never convince him nothing happened. He had to believe Mona. He died a broken man...broken in spirit and body. I lay that at Mona's feet."

Fancy trembled beneath his touch.

"You didn't know, did you, that Mona didn't call me when my father was ill? She didn't let me know until it was too late for me to be there. I arrived in time for the funeral, which was blessedly brief. If I'd had to spend time with that woman...I don't know what I would have done. She ruined my father, then wouldn't let him go. She stayed married to him hoping to still get his estate. Can you understand why I hated her so much?"

His fingers caressed Fancy's skin. She was torn in two directions, wanting his touch yet shrinking from it.

"I know why you're here, Fancy. You're here to use me to get what you can from Mona's estate. I bet it was quite a surprise when you found out the will Mona had made when she married Kurt was still in effect. When you found out I'm the executor. If I fell in love with you, you'd be just that much more certain of getting what you want, wouldn't you?"

"No," she whispered. "It's not like that."

He ignored her protest. "It won't work, Fancy. I'm one step ahead of you. This time your luscious body won't buy what you want."

Fancy rocked with the accusation. She backed away, scooting away from Rader carefully, watching the taut features of his face. The cold core grew inside her, taking the place of the exciting passion she'd found in his arms.

"I—it wasn't like that at all," she repeated. How could she make him believe that she'd known all along that he was the executor of Mona's estate. How could she explain that she'd used that information to have an opportunity to see him again, to test the residual feelings she harbored for him.

For long minutes, they stared at each other as adversaries. Fancy watched the rise and fall of his broad chest as Rader fought to control his breathing. His dark eyes glittered angrily in the firelight playing over his dark skin.

He knelt in front of her. His throat moved when he swallowed. Her chest felt as though she hadn't breathed in hours.

"What are we going to do, Fancy?" He threw his head back and stared at the ceiling. His hands rested on his thighs as his eyes closed in a silent anguish that marked his face.

"I don't know, Rader," she whispered. "I wish I knew."

Shivering slightly in the cooling room, she sat up and reached for the shirt. With trembling hands she began to untangle the sleeves.

"Fancy."

She flinched away from his voice. She didn't want to be reminded of what had almost happened. Examining it would make it far too real.

She flinched again when his hand fell upon her hip, his thumb falling on the pink scar on her stomach that peeped out above the bikini panties she wore.

"What's this?"

Fancy attempted to move away, but he would not allow it.

"Nothing. Please... I want to go upstairs."

"Fancy." The command drew her around.

"It's nothing insidious. Just an appendectomy scar."

"When?"

"What difference does it make?"

Her reluctance to answer his simple question alerted him. "It makes a difference to me. Was it recent?"

The scar was pink, new. Not more than a few weeks old. He wondered if it was the cause of the occasional twinge of discomfort he'd caught on her face and the times he'd seen her hand rest protectively on her stomach.

"It has nothing to do with you. Nothing about me has anything to do with you," she said bitterly.

"I wish that was the truth," he shot back.

The silence between them was heavy. The only sound was that of the receding storm, the thunder rumbling out across the valley as the clouds disappeared over the rim of the bluffs.

"Are we at an impasse?"

Fancy swallowed back tears threatening to clog her throat. "I guess so. You never fail to remind me what kind of woman Mona was. And how much I remind you of her. How could you stand to make love to me when you hate her so much?" She crushed the shirt to her chest, shaking her head. "I'm sorry. I didn't want things to be like this. None of it makes any sense."

Rader studied her, trying to sort truth from lies. What he saw and sensed confused him. Everything about her seemed genuine. Could he have been that wrong about her?

"Fancy, a lot of things don't make sense. But I intend to find out about them. With or without your help."

When Fancy didn't respond, Rader released her. With jerky movements that betrayed the ragged state of her nerves, Fancy pulled on the shirt and zipped her jeans. Then rising shakily to her feet, she fled the room, tears finally spilling over and down her cheeks.

Rader picked up her abandoned guitar, his thumb sliding over the strings as he followed the sound of her footsteps as Fancy ran upstairs. The sound of her door closing firmly echoed in the empty house.

"This isn't the end of it, Fancy," he said to the darkness. "It's only the beginning."

Chapter Nine

Fancy answered the telephone in the kitchen.

"Fancy?"

"Hi, Paul."

"There's a concert tonight at The Barn. Want to go?"

Fancy was hesitant, but didn't want to stay around the house, either. In the few days since she and Rader had almost made love, she'd spent her time avoiding him. He spent more and more time away from the house, too. Still, it seemed she was more aware of him than ever.

While their situation seemed at a standstill, she knew Rader had spoken to Brian on the telephone several times and had received registered mail from him. A nagging suspicion that those conversations and correspondence were about her kept returning. She wished he hadn't seen the scar. It had made him ask more questions. Questions she couldn't answer without seeming to be exactly who he thought she was—Mona's double.

"What time?"

"Well, the music doesn't start until about seven-thirty, but how about dinner before that? Give you strength for playing."

A smile lifted the corner of her mouth. "I thought this was a concert."

"It is. You're on the program."

Her heart warmed. It felt good to be wanted. To be a part of something that created enjoyment for people. "Okay. It sounds good to me."

"Great. I'll pick you up about six and we'll catch a bite at a café somewhere."

"Anything's fine with me."

There was a slight hesitation before Paul spoke again. "Are you all right? You sound a little down."

"I'm okay. I just need to get out of the house for a while."

"Are you sure? Mom says you and Rader have been sidling around one another like static electricity. Something going on?"

"No, Paul. It's nothing unusual. Rader's opinions of me haven't changed, and I think he's making sure we don't run into one another. Besides, he and Sharon have been together the last several nights—"

"Sharon hasn't been with Rader."

Fancy was surprised. "She hasn't? He's been out. I just assumed... Well, it has nothing to do with me."

"Sure you don't want to talk about it?"

"I'm sure. Things are just a little tense here while we're waiting for Mona's estate to be settled. When I leave, things will return to normal, I'm sure."

"Well, all right. But I'm here if you need someone to talk to."

"Thanks, Paul. I appreciate that."

"Anyway, you're on for tonight. Bring that guitar, okay?"

"Okay."

She hung up the phone, letting her hand rest on the receiver as she stared out the window into the early-afternoon sunlight. She couldn't believe it was the Fourth of July already. A day for celebrating freedom. She flexed her shoulders wearily. She definitely wasn't in a holiday mood.

"Was that Paul?"

Fancy spun around. Rader stood in the doorway where he had obviously been standing long enough to overhear at least part of her conversation.

"Yes."

"What did he want?"

Fancy drew a deep breath of resignation. As long as she was in his house, Rader would always feel he had a right to pry. "He invited me to a concert."

"You and he are dating?"

"No. Not really."

Passing a hand over her forehead in a gesture of utter weariness, Fancy swayed on her feet. Fatigue from sleepless nights again marked her eyes with faint shadows. She was so tired of this whole charade. But once again, she drew at the well of her fast-fading pride.

"You're going to the concert with him tonight?"

"Yes." Why couldn't Rader just leave her alone?

"On that motorcycle?"

Fancy glanced up in surprise. "Yes. Why?"

"It doesn't bother you? The appendectomy?"

A faint smile touched her generous mouth. "Rader, I've been riding that bike with Paul for weeks. I'm fine."

His eyes narrowed in speculation. "When did you have the surgery, Fancy?"

If she told him the truth, he'd connect it with the date of Mona's death, which would create a chain reaction of revelations she couldn't afford. She chose to ignore his question and use words as a defense.

"I have to get ready. Paul will be here about six. I have to shower and shampoo my hair. It takes forever to dry. See you later, Rader."

She escaped, but not before seeing the angry glint in his eyes.

Paul was prompt. Fancy gladly hopped behind him on the motorcycle, hugging the guitar close. They ate at a small, quaint restaurant where the simple menu offered delicious spaghetti.

Fancy ate with relish, wondering why everything tasted so good here. Maybe it had something to do with the fresh air or the company. Or maybe it was just that everything in San Francisco had begun to take on the flavor of the tasteless existence her life had become. She pushed the threatening depression away. Tonight was to enjoy, just for herself.

The Barn was just that—a converted barn. There was a raised platform at one end, and when Fancy and

Paul arrived, several musicians were already tuning up. Fancy was reluctant to put herself forward and hung back until a couple of the men she'd played with in Eureka Springs beckoned her onstage and introduced her to the others.

If it seemed strange to anyone that a woman was joining the group, their doubts were soon dispelled when Fancy began to play. She'd practiced for hours, carrying her guitar out into the woods to play alone whenever Rader was in the house. The practice showed. She picked up variations as though they were second nature now, and wide grins split old faces when a particularly intricate tune pattern developed.

The Barn filled with hoots and foot stomping to accompany the applause and show the appreciation of the audience. A tip of the hat from a fellow musician was enough to swell Fancy's heart with indefinable joy.

As the evening progressed Fancy glowed. She became totally oblivious to the audience. Her attention focused upon the music, her guitar and her fellow musicians. Whenever they dropped out for her to play a solo, she threw herself into it with vigor, her foot tapping the beat with a sharp staccato.

Her calloused fingers flew over the strings and it seemed she became more alive, more vibrant, as the evening progressed.

By ten o'clock, Fancy was exhausted. Sweat trickled down her back and between her breasts. She blotted her shirt against the dampness as the crowd finally began to disperse. Congratulations were abundant and warm from the men on the platform and from the audience. Fancy basked in their appreciation of her talent.

At last, Paul broke up the group around Fancy. "Ready to go? It's getting late and you look like you're wrung out."

She sent him a saucy grin. "Now that's a compliment I don't hear every day."

Paul held up his hands in mock surrender. "No offense, no offense. You're never less than lovely, but you do have this habit of throwing everything into the music. After three hours without a break, I figure it's time to call it a night."

She smiled at his uncharacteristically demanding tone. "I'm ready, believe me."

Saying her goodbyes, Fancy followed Paul outside.

"Did you see Rader and Sharon? They came in late and stood at the back until it started winding down. It's the first time I've seen them come to something like this. Can't say it's Sharon's cup of tea. She sees herself as the symphony type."

Fancy hadn't seen Rader, but was certain now he'd overheard her whole telephone conversation with Paul. Still, she wondered why he'd come. Was he so suspicious of her that he felt he had to follow her to the concert?

Paul parked the cycle in front of the house and walked Fancy to the door. "Rader and Sharon must not be back yet. Will you be all right here alone?"

"Sure. I like it when the house is quiet. It's something I rarely get to experience in the city. There's always hustle and bustle. I thoroughly believe the theory about noise pollution being harmful to your health."

Fancy was leaning against the door frame, and Paul lounged across from her. "Do you have to go back?"

Fumbling with her key, Fancy looked up. "Yes, I do. Paul, you know I'm only here for a kind of vacation. After that, I'll go back." She shrugged. "It seems to be a case of the sooner the better."

"I don't understand. I thought Rader's father had been married to your mother. That you were brother and sister, in a sense. At least, that's how Sharon explained it."

"True, but we're not really related. Our respective parents married when I was nearly eleven and Rader was, oh, almost twenty. He was in college, very idealistic, very intense, and he loved his father very much. He resented my mother, and I have to admit he had every reason to. Even though both are now deceased, Rader can't forget what Mona did to his father and to him."

"Is that what's wrong between the two of you?"

She was immediately wary. "What do you mean, 'wrong'?"

Paul shrugged. "No one can be around the two of you for very long without recognizing that there are sparks. I can tell you Sharon has noticed it." He studied Fancy in the shadows for a moment. "Is there anything I can do to help?"

Leaning back against the door, a small smile curved Fancy's lips. "Just be my friend, Paul. I value that more than anything."

Paul straightened a little, moving closer. "Then it won't matter if I claim just one kiss, will it? Just between friends?"

In answer, Fancy moved closer, her hand on his broad shoulder, and raised her lips to his.

In that moment, automobile lights swung across the yard, catching the two of them in the beams. The lights were not switched off until Fancy stepped back from Paul. She turned her face away from the light, knowing Rader had to be the new arrival. She could guess the interpretation he would put upon the scene he'd just witnessed.

Paul's hand was still on her arm when Rader approached. Hoping to avoid a scene, Fancy turned the key, which was still in the lock, and threw open the door.

"Thanks for tonight, Paul. I really enjoyed myself."

"I'll talk to you tomorrow. Take care."

"Good night."

She heard Rader's curt greeting to Paul, then the roar of the motorcycle as Paul pulled away from the house. Before she could escape upstairs, Rader stopped her.

"Fancy, I want to talk to you."

She hesitated with her foot on the second step. "I'm tired, Rader. Can't this wait until morning?"

"No. I'd rather take care of it now."

With weary resignation, Fancy followed Rader to his study. Her gaze avoided the fireplace and the rug in front of it. The memories were too poignant. Her foolishness still too fresh.

Fancy hesitated in the middle of the room before finally sitting on the couch.

"I want to compliment you. That was quite a performance tonight. Those people were eating out of your hands."

She frowned up at him. "What are you really trying to say, Rader?"

"How long can you keep up this little charade? You've made yourself indispensable to Miriam here at the house. According to Sharon, Paul thinks you're the greatest thing that ever happened to the valley. Even those people at The Barn tonight have accepted you completely. To cap it off, the kids there thought you were Cinderella and Snow White wrapped up in one. Where will it end?"

Wearily, she pressed long fingers into her temples. "Rader, we keep having the same conversation. I don't want to hear it all again. I'm going upstairs."

When she started to get up, Rader was there. His arms braced on either side of her, pinning her against the back of the couch. "No, that's not all I wanted to discuss. I want to talk about the other night."

"There's nothing to talk about."

"I think there is. I want to know how you feel about...about everything." Rader had thought about what happened until his head spun. He just couldn't get everything to click into place. What he saw, what he knew, and the questions still unanswered all added up to a puzzle that just wouldn't go together. He had to know what she was all about, but he didn't like having to ask her.

"What makes you think I have any feelings about it?"

His muscles tensed. "Damn you," he whispered into her face. "Talk to me!"

"About what?" Fancy tossed back. "About how it felt to have the great R. C. Malone in my arms? Or how it felt to have him compare me to a woman he openly admits he hates? Sorry, Rader. I don't kiss and tell."

"What's between you and Paul?"

Fancy lifted an eyebrow in mocking question. "No more than you saw tonight . . . and less. We shared a casual kiss. A kiss between friends. Do you understand that word? *Friends?*"

He ignored her sarcasm. "Is that what he'll say when I ask him?"

Fancy's lips tightened in anger. "Oh, come on, Rader. Not even you would be that crass. After all, you're not my father."

For a long tense moment, Rader's angry gaze met hers. She fought the urge to push him aside and escape. But then Rader made his move.

The cushions of the couch sank as Rader balanced his weight upon them and leaned over her. Before Fancy could think, his mouth brushed her cheek, nuzzling the sensitive flesh beneath her ear. Waves of sensation surged through her.

She let her head roll back against the couch, allowing him free access to the soft curve of her jaw and throat. No matter what happened, Rader could always reach her sensually. When he came into a room, her senses came alive, and when he touched her, every animosity was forgotten. This thing between them was crazy. But it was a wonderful craziness, and she surrendered to it.

"Fancy, you're a fever in my brain," he whispered. "I dream of holding you, making love to you. I can't get you out of my mind. I can't sleep. I can't work. I've tried to hate you . . . and I can't anymore."

His insistent body forced her back against the couch. The persuasion of his mouth erased the last remnants of reluctance to surrender to his seduction.

"Rader . . ." Her breath choked in her constricted throat.

"Yes," he breathed. "Say my name. I want to hear it when I take you."

Her protest was lost beneath the assault of his kiss. She followed him as he slid her beneath him on the couch. Their legs tangled. She reached for him as he supported himself on arms braced on either side of her face. His lips brushed hers tauntingly. She answered his tantalization with tiny nips and felt the beat of his heart grow ragged beneath her sensitive palms.

Sliding her hands up around his neck, she buried her fingers in his hair, testing the crispness of it. Then she forced him back to her, catching his mouth with hers and beginning her own sensual assault. She'd suffered her own hours of sleeplessness and walking the floor. Now she could taste her dreams.

She slipped her fingers beneath his shirt to explore the smooth skin of his tapered back. Her reward was a feverish groan. "Fancy, you set me on fire. I'm mindless when I'm with you. I can't get enough of you."

Fancy stopped his words with her mouth, catching and holding it to force him to answer her passion. He relaxed over her, his chest crushing her aching breasts as he enveloped her in his strong arms.

His lips trailed kisses down the tender arch of her throat to the swell of her breast. Nuzzling aside her collar, his lips traced the provocative swell. She caught his face in her hands and brought his lips back to hers. She could never get enough of him.

Rader's nimble fingers released the buttons of her shirt in a tantalizing slowness. Rivers of pleasure undulated through her body. His hand was at the snap of her jeans and she was surging against him when the sharp ring of the telephone stabbed into the room.

They were both frozen in disbelief. Suddenly Rader relaxed against her, his head resting in the hollow of her shoulders. The knuckles of his hand bore into the soft pillow of her stomach.

"Oh, God," he groaned against her.

Fancy's mind and body echoed his frustration.

Finally, Rader reached out and lifted the receiver and rolled away from her. When he answered the phone, Fancy relaxed a moment before pulling herself erect. Then she stood and headed for the door. Passion was gone and in its place, logic reigned.

"Fancy, don't go."

She didn't turn around. He might see too much in her face. "I can't stay, Rader. I've made enough mistakes."

For a long moment he said nothing. Just looked at her.

"Brian will be here at the end of the week. He wants to talk to you."

That made her turn around. His shirt hung open and his hair lay in abandon across his forehead. The telephone receiver rested against his shoulder, the caller waiting.

"Why?"

"I asked him to look into a few things for me."

She swallowed. "What things?"

"I told you I'd find out about you, Fancy."

"You had me investigated? How could you do that? You had no right!"

Rader's eyes darkened in speculation. "But I do have that right. I'm saddled with the job of executor of Mona's estate. I have every right to find out what I'm dealing with."

Fancy could only stare at him in disbelief. "I didn't realize how much you really hated me."

Long fingers covered her trembling lips. She turned and ran from the room, leaving Rader staring after her uncomprehendingly.

What is it, Fancy? Rader asked the retreating figure. What are you so afraid of me finding out?

Chapter Ten

Fancy went downstairs reluctantly the next morning. After forcing down a breakfast of toast and coffee, she wandered outside. Warm sunshine caressed her face, clearing her mind of the muzziness of a sleepless night.

Strolling around to the back of the house, she spied the horse barn. Having never gone that direction before, Fancy meandered toward the weathered wood structure.

Inside, the odors of horses, hay and grain assailed her senses. It was a comforting smell, and she stepped inside eagerly. Three animals pushed their heads over their stalls. A black and two bays seemed to be the sole occupants.

"Hello, fella. You're a beauty." She rubbed the nose of the black. He tossed his head nervously, and she moved on to the other two.

"And how are you, pretty lady?" she rubbed at the blaze down the face of the first bay. She was smaller than the black and compactly built.

More friendly than the black, the matching bays nuzzled together, pushing into Fancy's hand for attention. She laughed delightedly at their antics.

"They're insufferable, wanting constant attention. They're hoping you have sugar for them."

Fancy tensed at the sound of Rader's baritone coming from the darkness of the loft. Forcing herself to turn slowly, she looked up at him. "I didn't know you were here."

Rader crouched in the loft opening. "Obviously not. You would have avoided the place like the plague."

"Can you blame me? All we do is fight."

"Not always." He quirked a smile at the slight flush that brushed her cheeks. "But there definitely is something volatile between us. Neither of us can deny it."

Throwing back her head, Fancy flexed tense muscles in her shoulders. "Then perhaps we should make certain to avoid one another." She turned aside. "I'll go back to the house."

"Fancy, wait."

She halted, shoulders hunched, hands shoved deeply into the back pockets of her jeans.

There was the thud of his boots striking the wood of the barn floor as he dropped from the loft.

"What do you want?"

"A truce?"

He stood behind her now, but Fancy refused to turn. "Truce?"

"You make it sound like a foreign word."

"It is between us."

There was a significant pause. "Yes, I guess it is."

"Then I'll go to the house and stay out of your way."

His fingers wrapped about her upper arm to draw her around to face him. "How about a truce for the day, then. Let's go for a ride. I can have Miriam pack a picnic for us and we can make a day of it."

She searched his face for ulterior motives. What she intended to say didn't come out. "I'd like that. But I don't ride well."

"No matter. We'll take it easy. I'd like you to see more of the valley."

Again she studied him, trying to read his thoughts. "All right."

"Good. What you have on is fine. I'll tell Miriam to fix the food and I'll meet you here in thirty minutes."

"Okay." Fancy escaped, needing the half hour to regather her shaken composure and ask herself why she'd agreed to the outing. Nothing was going as she'd planned.

An hour before noon, Fancy returned to the barn. Rader was already there. The black horse pranced nervously beside him while he finished tightening the cinch on one of the smaller mares.

"He's a beauty," Fancy commented as a way of introducing her arrival.

"Thanks. I don't get to ride him often enough and he's anxious to run."

"I still find it difficult to picture you in this rural scene."

Rader shrugged his broad shoulders. "We never did know one another well. Certainly not as adults."

She agreed. "No, though it hardly seems worth the effort now. Soon we'll go our separate ways and that will be the end of it."

"Will it?"

She slanted a glance at him. "Yes. That's best."

Rader adjusted the bridle carefully. "We have a truce, remember?"

"Do you think that's possible?"

"If we both want it."

Her teeth savaged her lower lip. Though reluctant to test the strength of the fragile truce, she was more adverse to being confined to the house again all day. "All right."

"Good." Rader swung into the saddle and easily controlled his mount. "Let's go."

Fancy put her foot into the stirrup and swung inexpertly into the saddle.

"Stirrups the right length?"

"They're fine."

"We'll take it easy until you're accustomed to handling her. We'll stop in a clearing I know of in about an hour and have lunch."

"I'm sure I'll be ready by then."

His dark gaze fell on her. "Are you sure this won't be too much for you?"

Her pale eyes met his. "If I get tired, I'll tell you. All right?"

"Okay, then. Let's go." Rader led out, urging the large black stallion forward.

Fancy followed, her gaze reluctantly resting in the middle of Rader's back. Strapped behind him was a flat wicker basket that held their lunch. His body moved easily with the rhythm of the black animal prancing under his control.

A flush stole over her body as Fancy watched the movement of man and horse, and she swiftly averted her eyes.

She concentrated, instead, on her surroundings. Rain had washed the countryside briefly just before dawn, leaving it fresh and green. Rader led them up the hill at the back of the house. Fancy leaned forward over the neck of her horse as they climbed.

Upon reaching the top, Rader reined in to allow Fancy to look down into a new section of the valley. The river widened, leaving gravel bars in evidence on both sides halfway down the valley. It was as though some painter had smeared his tube of brown paint on a lush green canvas.

In a moment, Rader moved on without comment. Fancy relaxed, enjoying the quiet, the peace. She lost herself in the vistas opening before her. It seemed only a few moments until he led them into the trees again.

They dodged low limbs. It was cooler in the shadows of the forest. Only the sounds of birds, a breeze and the creaking of their saddles in time with the clip-clop of horses' hooves broke the forest quiet.

A clearing opened before them. Rader swung off his horse and wrapped the reins around a low limb. Glancing up at her, Rader began unstrapping their lunch from behind his saddle.

"This is the place."

Now Fancy became aware of the strain placed upon her thighs by the unnatural seat. Resting her strained muscles, she swung her right leg over the saddle and stood beside her horse a moment. Her muscles quivered and she wondered if her legs would hold her.

"Are you all right?"

Fancy laughed. "I think so. Just a little shaky." She took a tentative step. "I'm all right. Where shall we spread the blanket?"

Rader gestured toward a sunny spot. "There. It's cool enough to make the sun feel good."

Fancy flipped out the blanket and opened the basket. Cold chicken, fresh, sliced tomatoes, cucumber spears and carrot sticks, and generously buttered homemade bread. Large thermos bottles held coffee and lemonade, and Miriam's specialty, large chocolate-chip cookies, completed the offering.

"Looks like Miriam has done herself proud."

Fancy glanced up at Rader's comment. "She is a marvelous cook."

"Can't see where her cooking has done anything toward putting meat on those bones of yours."

There was a teasing glint in his eyes that she responded to. "Don't you like my bones?"

The teasing look altered subtly. "Yeah, I like your bones."

Refusing to acknowledge the sensuality in his comment, Fancy continued laying out silverware. "Might be a song title in there somewhere."

Rader smiled. Perhaps this truce thing would work better than he'd expected. "Name a book title and I know it. But music isn't my forte."

"It's the opposite with me. I've read your books, though."

"And?"

She flashed him a smile. "Fishing for compliments?"

"Not from you," he acknowledged. "From you I want only the truth."

"Then the truth is, I liked your novels. You're very skillful at creating characters and advancing the plot. You make your people live. I found myself becoming angry with them, crying because of them and occasionally laughing with them. I wondered how much of you was in each story."

By now they'd filled their plates and settled down to eat. Rader sat with a chicken leg suspended between his plate and his mouth. "Was that important?"

Now she was caught. She couldn't afford to reveal how important it had been to her to keep in touch with him in even this remote way. So she lied. "Only in that . . . I had known you . . . for a time. Celebrity Syndrome or something." She took a bite of chicken breast.

"Was it?"

"Of course." She concentrated on dipping a carrot stick into a special dip Miriam had created.

He allowed the two words to fall unanswered between them. For several minutes they each concentrated upon the food. Finally Fancy spoke.

"What kind of story are you working on now?"

Rader laid aside the clean leg bone. "It's a novel about child pornography."

She glanced up in surprise. "Really? What prompted that theme?"

Shrugging, Rader helped her repack the basket. "Nothing personal, certainly." At her grin, he continued. "Just some information that fell into my hands while researching another book. I thought it was time to use it."

"How much of the book will be factual?"

They sat on the cleared blanket, more at ease with each other than she'd thought possible after the tension of the past weeks.

"The core of the story is true, or could be true. It's happened hundreds of times—runaways or children kidnapped and used. The rest is imagination."

Her wide pale gaze rested upon his strong face. "How do you make your characters come alive? That's the thing I noticed most in your books."

"I use the what-if theory."

"What if?"

"What if this happened to me? How would I feel? That sort of thing."

She nodded understandingly. "It's the same with music. You use experience, feelings, emotions, and translate them into notes on a scale, then you add words."

"Both create a story."

"Right."

"Then we have something in common."

She'd been looking deeply into the cool green shade of the forest, but at his comment, she glanced at Rader warily. "I suppose so. Isn't it time to ride again?"

He recognized her evasion. "Yes. I'd like you to see the floor of the valley." With that, he leaped agilely to his feet and pulled Fancy up beside him.

Their gazes met and held until she dropped hers. He accepted her refusal to meet his challenge. Rader strapped the basket and blanket on his horse. Fancy swung slowly onto her mount. Again Rader led the way.

By the time they reached the floor of the valley, Fancy's muscles were feeling the strain.

"Let's cross the river here."

Fancy nodded, unwilling to admit she was growing tired.

Rader's mount pranced nervously at walking onto the loose gravel bar, but Rader brought him under control again. He urged the horse forward, but the stallion's skitterishness transferred to Fancy's mount. Her grip on the reins tightened. She was feeling apprehensive.

Suddenly, the black plunged into the water, kicking up rocks and spray into the mare's face. The mare jumped sideways and Fancy slipped in the saddle. Grabbing for the saddlehorn, she clung to it as her mount plunged into the deeper water.

Rader was already halfway across the river, his concentration on keeping his mount under control. He glanced back once to see Fancy clinging to her saddle.

He started to call to her but just then his horse took another lunge.

Water splashed over his legs as the black lost his footing. Rader grimaced as water filled his boots, but he urged the horse forward relentlessly.

Fancy watched Rader's horse begin to fall, then right himself. Her mare was still jumpy but kept her feet, for which Fancy could only be grateful.

They finally reached the opposite shore. By now, the stallion had calmed. Rader stepped down and waited for Fancy.

"Looks like you nearly got a dunking," she said breathlessly, feeling fortunate at staying in the saddle herself.

He grinned engagingly. "Yeah. But I was worried about you. Let's stop so I can empty these boots."

Fancy giggled at the squishing sound when Rader walked. "Over there looks good." She pointed to the edge of the gravel bar where grass met the beginning of the forest.

Stepping down from her horse slowly, her muscles complaining, Fancy untied the blanket from Rader's horse. Flipping it open on the patch of grass, she sank down upon it with a loud sigh.

"Sore?" Rader dropped down beside her and began tugging at his boots.

"A little," she admitted.

Rader poured water from both boots and stripped off sodden socks. Fancy giggled as he wrung them out. The creases beside his mouth deepened when he grinned at her.

"My fault. Haven't had a chance to exercise him much the last few weeks and the riverbed is rocky and uncertain there. I'd forgotten."

"I'm just glad you didn't lose him. My horse would have followed, and I'm not sure I could have handled her."

She picked up the wad he'd made of his socks and carefully spread them out in the sun.

"You did okay."

"Yeah, but you gave me a gentle mount. Saved my neck."

Their gazes met and the pretense fell away. The sun was warm on her skin, the grass green and fragrant. The rippling water was the music. What she felt for Rader provided the words.

Unconsciously, Fancy swayed toward Rader and he reached for her. His hand slipped beneath her braid, clasping her neck at the base of her skull to draw her mouth to his.

Closing her eyes, Fancy closed her mind to everything except the feel of his lips on hers. She breathed in, absorbing the woodsy aroma of his cologne, the male smell of him tainted by a horsey odor that was not unpleasant. When he urged her closer, she went.

Their mutual response was immediate. Their appetite tempted by their passionate fireside encounter, further tested by a morning spent in easy companionship, made for an explosive situation. They were greedy for each other. The flow of the river became one with the flow of passion within them.

Rader rolled to his back, drawing Fancy over him. She adjusted her body to his, resting her cheek on his broad chest, cradled in his hips by his raised leg. Unconsciously, she moved against him, seeking to be still nearer.

Her arms slid around his shoulders. Rader rolled her over, his urgent body covering hers. His mouth covered hers in a deep kiss that shook her very soul. A kind of desperation enveloped her. She wanted him, needed his passion, his love, to fulfill the unrealized dreams of her life.

But even as his fingers were at the buttons of her shirt, she resurrected reality. She'd come to find herself, to find out whether she and Rader could find something together. But whatever they found, it had to be more than sex. It had to be something deeper.

"No, Rader. Please..."

"Fancy, don't say that...." His mouth hushed her protest.

She pushed at his shoulders. "No. Please, Rader. I—I can't."

"Yes," he urged against her lips. "Yes."

She turned her face aside to deny the passion tearing at her. He would never understand. Not even if she could tell him the reasons for her erratic actions.

"I'm sorry."

The words were whispered as she closed her eyes. She was sorry for so many things. Sorry she couldn't accept this momentary pleasure; sorry there was so much pain and mistrust between them. But Rader naturally misinterpreted.

Rolling to his feet he began to shove his shirt into his jeans. "Hell!" he breathed, his gaze sweeping over her again. Stamping on his damp boots, he strode toward the tethered horses.

Fancy lay still for a moment, willing the tears stinging her eyes not to fall. Finally she rose, rolled up the blanket, including Rader's socks, and walked to her horse.

They rode home in silence, both involved in their own thoughts. When they got back to the barn, Fancy left the horses in his care and went to the house for a hot bath and a long cry. Tomorrow, Brian would arrive, and she had no idea what would happen then.

Chapter Eleven

Dawn brushed the sky before Fancy fell into a fitful sleep. She'd worried the subject of what Brian would tell Rader until she could no longer even think. It was late when she awoke. Some perverse nature made her dress in her oldest T-shirt and most-faded jeans. Brushing her hair back, she braided it loosely to fall down her back.

Miriam Sartin was at her post in the kitchen. "I just want coffee, Miriam. I have some things to do outside today."

"You'll always be skinny as a rail if you keep on this way, girl. Oh, there was a phone call for you earlier. I left the number there by the telephone. They said it was very important you call."

"Thanks." Fancy picked up the number and stared at it, not recognizing it though it had a San Francisco area code. She went into the study to use the phone there in privacy. Sipping coffee, she dialed the number and asked for a Mr. Leonard.

"Miss Connors?"

"Yes."

"Miss Connors, much as I hate doing this, we're going to have to take legal action against you for the unpaid balance on your hospital and surgical fees. We've attempted to contact you several times to no avail...."

A frown creased her forehead. "Just who are you, Mr. Leonard? What is this number?"

"A-1 Collection Agency. We're retained by the hospital to collect past-due accounts, Miss Connors."

"But I made payment arrangements...."

"Arrangements that are unsatisfactory, Miss Connors. This is quite a large outstanding bill. We must have payment in full at this point or you'll be served—"

"But there's nothing else I can do." Panic flooded through Fancy. She stammered, trying to think of a way to delay legal action of any kind. "B-because of the circumstances I explained in my letter to the hospital, I had to leave San Francisco. Above that, my doctor hasn't released me to work. I can't return to the coast or to work until late this summer at the earliest. There's nothing more I can do. Taking me to court will only increase the obligation with additional legal fees." She hated pleading. "Surely you can understand my position."

"Of course, but we're employed to collect money, Miss Connors. We've gone past our normal waiting

period now because of the situation you've explained.''

Now his voice was sounding oily and Fancy knew
total defeat. He wasn't about to listen to her.

''We can do no more. We're obligated to our client
to see that these bills are paid. Surely there are some
arrangements you can make. Borrow the money. Perhaps some member of your family can help.''

Desperation sharpened her voice. ''Don't you think
I've thought of that? I've tried everything I can think
of. I exhausted all those possibilities before I left San
Francisco.'' She paced the floor as she pleaded, long
fingers stroking her aching forehead. ''I promise you,
Mr. Leonard, that as soon as I can I'll get the money.
There's just no way I can do anything right now.''

''I'm sorry, Miss Connors. I really am. The account will be turned over to the attorney at the end of
the week. If you can come to some other arrange-
ment, you can call me at this number. Otherwise,
you'll be hearing from our attorney.''

Fancy's shoulders slumped. ''I understand.''

She replaced the receiver and sank into a chair, her
head in her hands.

''Miriam said you had an important call. Is something wrong?''

The temptation to tell Rader everything was strong,
but she couldn't risk that.

''No, nothing. Nothing that my having never come
here couldn't solve.''

She ran past him out of the room and up the stairs.

Rader stared after her, then bent and picked up a piece of paper with a telephone number printed across it. Folding it, he slipped it into his pocket.

Fancy paced the floor of her room, her arms wrapped protectively about her middle as she tried to think of a way out of her problems. In her rational mind, she knew she should tell Rader everything and take the consequences. But if she did, it would mean she'd accepted that there was no hope for her and Rader. She couldn't make herself give that up just yet.

Perhaps she could work something out with Brian. Perhaps borrow against the estate. But if she told Brian anything, he'd be sure to tell Rader. Then there would be hell to pay. Asking for money would only verify Rader's suspicions of her. They'd come so close. So close.

Finally, Fancy couldn't stay in the room any longer and ran downstairs. "Miriam, I'm going for a walk. I'll be back in an hour or so, if anyone asks."

"You be careful. The sky's looking funny. Might be a tornado brewing."

Fancy dismissed the warning. "I'll watch the clouds."

"Be sure you do," Miriam called. "There's warnings on the radio—" But Fancy was already out the door and out of hearing.

Fancy walked for a long time. Quite often, she explored the woods, careful to always keep her directions straight so she wouldn't get lost. But today she was distracted. Today she walked to escape the inevitable.

She strode, long-legged and loose, through woods and clearings. She stopped and tasted crisply cold spring water when she was thirsty, touched the delicate petals of woodland flowers. She climbed the fallen half of a tree that had been struck by lightning years before to look through the sun-dappled trees.

Part of her loved this place. Cherished its peace and simplicity. Yet a part of her was homesick. Homesick for Alfonso, for the music, her students. For the people she played for each night at Rolando's. Even for The Blue Note. It hadn't always been easy, but it had been her life. She missed its familiarity. The mind-occupying routine.

It wasn't everything, but it would have to be enough. What she'd hoped for—Rader's love—wasn't going to be hers. She had to accept that.

The day had wound down to late afternoon before Fancy came to herself. She'd been wandering for hours and now had no idea where she was. Momentary panic flooded her before she calmed herself and forced some logic to the surface. Looking skyward through the trees she couldn't see the sun in any direction.

Sometime during her wandering, clouds had come up and the horizon, what she could see of it, was darkening. Only now did she realize that she could no longer hear sounds of forest creatures. The birds were silent and the breeze in the treetops had taken on a strangely keening sound.

Miriam's warning echoed in her mind, and Fancy realized how foolish she had been not to be more aware of weather changes.

Find an opening, a clearing, the edge of the trees, Fancy told herself. Find some way to orient yourself. Get a direction. She kept repeating those instructions to herself to still rising panic.

Fancy kept walking, not allowing herself the luxury of the tears that threatened. In the back of her mind nagged the realization that no one knew where she was or what direction she'd taken.

When the first sprinkles of rain came through the closely intertwined leaves of the trees, Fancy returned to awareness. Her situation was serious. The wind that had been so gentle was now high, bending the trees and breaking limbs. The clouds were low and rolling. Flashes of lightning could be seen and heard. The close-growing trees were shedding some of the rain but, by the sound, she knew it was coming down in torrents. Once again, the unpredictability of an Ozarks summer had proven itself.

Fancy was soon soaked to the skin. Her thin T-shirt clung to her, and she began to shake from cold. She looked for shelter, but there was none. She realized she was probably walking in circles.

Shivering uncontrollably, Fancy sank down at the foot of a tree. Wrapping her arms about herself, she rested her head on drawn-up knees. The rain ran in rivulets down her face, plastering her hair to her head and back. Her jeans were heavy and cold, her boots stiff and shrinking. Hopelessness enveloped her.

Surrendering to fatigue, she curled into a ball and lay down between the heavy curling roots of the tall oak. She tried to convince herself someone would come looking for her, and failed.

She had no idea how long she lay beneath the tree with her eyes closed, rain washing her face. Her body was wracked with tremors but her mind did not register the cold. Then, as if from a very far place, she heard her name being called. But when she tried to respond, her voice came out a whisper.

The call was repeated and Fancy forced herself up to a seated position. Her teeth chattered so badly she clenched her jaws. When the call came again, Fancy pushed against the tree trunk and stood shakily. She tried calling out but failed.

Then she saw a fallen limb. Grasping it in both hands she began pounding it against the tree trunk.

Two men in bright yellow slickers burst through the edge of the trees into the clearing. She saw them but kept pounding on the tree trunk, the dull thud a rhythm.

"Fancy, it's all right. You're found." Rader forced her fingers to unwrap from the limb. "Paul, call in the others. Take them down to the house for coffee and sandwiches. I'll bring Fancy in myself. Make sure the doctor's there."

The second figure sent a quick nod in Rader's direction before trotting off into the trees. She heard three short blasts on a whistle repeated twice and vaguely realized it was a prearranged signal.

"How...how did..." Her whisper was lost when Rader picked her up.

"Miriam said you'd gone walking. When you didn't return by lunch, she became worried and called me."

"I'm sorry," Fancy whispered. "I didn't mean to get lost. I just wanted to think...."

"Hush, now. There's plenty of time to talk later."

Fancy's head rested against his shoulder as she let darkness take her.

Rader mounted the stairs and carried Fancy into his own room. "I'm going to run a hot shower and I want you to stay in it until you're warmed through. Do you understand me?"

Fancy nodded.

"Miriam is heating some soup."

While he talked, Rader stripped off Fancy's wet clothes. She clung to his broad shoulders gratefully while he pulled off her boots and sodden jeans.

Steam began to float in the air before Rader thrust her unceremoniously beneath the hot spray. The heat felt wonderful. Bracing herself against two walls, Fancy bowed her head to let the hot water flow over her shoulders and back.

She was still standing under the water when the shower door opened and Rader thrust a steaming cup of broth inside. "Drink that and stay in there."

The chicken broth tasted wonderful and its warmth threaded through her body like tiny rivulets of heat. Finally Rader reached inside and turned off the shower. When she stepped out, he wrapped her in a warm bath sheet and briskly dried her.

"Rader, I can do that myself," she protested.

"Be quiet, woman. You're chilled to the bone. Here, swallow these."

He handed her two tablets and a glass of water and waited until she swallowed the aspirin.

"Come on. It's bed for you."

She didn't protest. She was exhausted, and going to sleep sounded wonderful. Rader pushed her arms into the overly large sleeves of a pajama top and towel dried her hair. By the time he was satisfied her hair was dry enough, Fancy was drooping.

She really didn't remember getting into bed. Later, she was vaguely aware that there was someone in bed with her and she curled into the warmth. Arms came around her and pulled her close. Feeling safe, comforted, Fancy immediately fell into a deep sleep.

When Fancy awoke again, her throat felt scratchy. Her eyes felt heavy and gritty, and her face was hot. A cough choked its way past her sore throat, and she struggled to sit up to ease the heaviness in her chest.

Cool fingers lay against her cheek and a glass was placed against her lips. She drank automatically, thirstily, and fell asleep again.

When she awoke, sunlight was streaming through the window. She rolled onto her back to find Rader sitting at the bedside, watching her.

"Well, Sleeping Beauty, how about some broth and juice."

Though her head felt loggy, her nose stuffy, Fancy felt a little better. "Soup?"

"Miriam has some simmering on the stove. Would you like to get up for a moment?"

At her nod, he pulled back the covers and helped her slide out of bed. When she swayed, Rader scooped her into his arms and carried her to the bathroom.

"Will you be all right if I leave you for a few minutes?"

At her nod, he pulled the door open and disappeared.

When she finished, she started back to the bed on her own. Just as she got to the bed, Rader came in carrying a tray. The aroma of soup made her stomach growl with hunger.

"You're pampering me."

"I could get used to doing that."

Fancy frowned but Rader ignored her. Settling her against the pillows, he brought the tray and balanced it while she sipped hot soup from a fat mug.

"Later, if you're feeling better, I'll carry you downstairs."

She stared into the cup, trying to find the right words to say thank you. "Rader, I'm sorry I caused so much trouble."

"Why did you go walking when there was a storm threatening?"

"I had to get away." She shrugged. "I guess I thought I could walk away all my troubles. It didn't work. I just made more."

"Well, some of them are gone. Why didn't you tell me how sick you were?"

"What do you mean?"

"Fancy, stop going in circles. I talked to your doctor." At her frown, he explained. "I found your medication on your night stand. When Dr. Walker came after I brought you in, he phoned your doctor in San Francisco to see what other kind of medicines you might be taking so he could prescribe an antibiotic."

"I see." If he'd found her doctor, it wouldn't be long until he knew the rest.

"Here, take your medicine and get some more sleep."

Her eyes did feel heavy and her head was muzzy again. She couldn't think at all. As she fell asleep, the last thing Fancy saw was Rader's face as he leaned over to brush back tendrils of hair from her face. His touch was so tender. If she could only think maybe she could figure out why he was being so gentle with her when he should be so angry.

It was a long time later when Fancy awoke. Rader was nowhere in sight. Dusk had fallen and she was thirsty. Pushing herself up on an elbow, she reached for the carafe of water on the night stand. But her hand trembled, knocking the glass onto the floor. Rader immediately appeared in the doorway.

"Fancy?" When he saw what she was attempting, a frown of exasperation crossed his face. "Couldn't you call if you wanted something? Do you always have to be so independent?"

Pouring a glass of water for her, he held it while Fancy drank. The ice water tasted wonderful. She relaxed gratefully against the pillow after drinking her fill.

"Well, you're awake at last." A stranger stood in the doorway. "I'm Dr. Walker. You weren't conscious when I was here yesterday."

He approached the bed, and Fancy sent Rader a questioning look.

"You were out of it a whole day and I called the doctor again."

"I'm fine...." Fancy protested feebly. She'd had enough of hospitals.

"We'll just see about that," Dr. Walker said as he unsnapped his bag. "Let me listen to your chest."

Dr. Walker was efficient, listening to her breathing front and back while Rader watched.

"So far, everything sounds all right. There's a little congestion, but nothing too worrisome. Rest, drink lots of liquids and take the antibiotics I prescribed." He packed away his stethoscope. "You're very lucky, considering your condition before this happened."

At Fancy's wary look, the doctor continued. "Yes, I've spoken to Dr. Frazier. From what we—" he gestured to Rader "—can determine you haven't obeyed his instructions very well. You haven't been taking your vitamins, have you? And, I'd guess you only take your ulcer medication when you need it. Right?" At her look, he nodded in confirmation. "How's your stomach feeling?"

"It's okay."

"Humm. Now, tomorrow you can begin going downstairs for an hour or so. But I want you to get plenty of bed rest. And I want you to take *all* your medication. I'll see you at the beginning of the week."

With those instructions, the doctor sent Rader a salute and strode briskly out of the room.

"Are you going to mind this time?"

Fancy licked her dry, cracked lips. "I guess so. I have little choice, don't I?"

Rader stood at the foot of the bed. "Fancy, why? Why didn't you tell me you'd just gotten out of the hospital?"

She picked at the hem of the blanket, avoiding his glowering look. "I didn't think it was any of your concern."

He paced the floor agitatedly. "Why are you so stubborn! I could have made things easier for you. Instead of badgering you, I could have made sure you were taking care of yourself."

"I've been taking care of myself for a long time now, Rader. Everything just happened at the wrong time, that's all."

Rader leaned over Fancy, his arms braced on either side of her as she sank back against the pillows. "Yes, they did. And I'm partly to blame for that, aren't I? I'm a lot to blame for you going out yesterday and getting lost." A muscle in his jaw jumped with tension. "I'm sorry, honey. I'm sorry for everything."

She started to protest, but he waved away her retort. "If I'd checked things out before, if I'd not jumped to conclusions... Never mind. We'll talk about everything when you're feeling better. Maybe then I can find some way to deal with the guilt I have for my part in what's happened to you."

She didn't understand completely. But she was certain now that Rader didn't know quite everything. If he did, he wouldn't be so nice to her. He'd be angry instead of apologetic. Brian must not have come yet with his reports.

"Could you drink another cup of soup? That's all the doctor will let you have today."

She answered absently, her thoughts occupied with how much Rader might know about her and about Mona. "That would be nice."

When Rader left to get the soup, Fancy pulled the covers up to her chin again and tried to think through everything Rader had told her. After she drank the soup, she fell asleep again.

Later in the day, Rader carried her downstairs to the couch in the study.

"You make a great nurse."

"There are—" he grinned "—certain advantages to dispensing medicine and taking temperatures."

"Humm," she said, snuggling into the blanket. "I don't like being sick, but the medicine does give everything a wonderfully misty feeling. I think I like that."

His warm breath fanned her cheek as he tucked her in. "Reality will rear its ugly head in a couple of days, but I'll be with you this time. I won't leave you alone again."

Her head rolled toward him on the pillows. "What do you mean?"

His lips brushed her cheek as he sat on the edge of the couch and leaned over her. "That's part of what we have to talk about. But that's for later."

Chapter Twelve

"I don't understand," Fancy said warily.

He brushed her hair back from her face gently and a warm, comfortable feeling spread through her body. He leaned toward her and then, almost reluctantly, as if testing her receptivity, his lips pressed against hers once, twice.

She reached for him, her fingers burying themselves in the thatch of his hair and holding him to her as she nibbled at his lips. Finally, he took her mouth in the aggressive fashion that was Rader Malone.

"I want you," he breathed. "You know that...."

"Rader," she whispered. "Love me. I just need you to love me, hold me. I won't ask anything more of you. I just want tonight...this minute.... Make me feel...."

"Baby, if you only knew how I felt right now." His voice was low, husky, caressing.

She clung to him, drawing him closer. The cushions shifted as he slid onto the couch beside her. Fancy turned on her side to allow Rader more room. Though the blankets separated them, Fancy could feel the heat radiating from his body and the heavy, measured beat of his heart against her as he crushed her to him.

"I shouldn't be doing this. Not now. You're not up to it. But I need to hold you."

"Umm, this feels good." Fancy relaxed against him.

"Talk to me," he whispered.

"Actions speak louder than words," she murmured teasingly, loving the new truce between them. She wasn't going to think about what had instigated it. Not yet.

"I need to hear them. I need the words, just as I need you to touch me—as I need to touch you."

"Rader, you know I want you. When you touch me, I can't hide it."

"Then say it. Tell me what you feel, how I make you feel."

"You're a verbal man, Rader. You need the words. I need the music."

His lips brushed her forehead. "Alone the words are a poem, the music only a melody. Together they make the song, a symphony."

Her slim fingers worried a curl flat upon his chest. "That's how you make me feel—like a full-blown symphony. Like I'm soaring, flying above everything and everyone. I'm a melody on the wind, unfettered, free. When you hold me...it's the most incredible symphony ever experienced."

Rader gathered her to him, pressing her face into his shoulder. "That's what I needed. I can take your body, make you respond to me physically, but I needed to touch your soul. That place inside you no one has ever reached before."

The prospect of Rader wanting that much of her, needing that much of her, was overwhelming. It should have been a dream come true. Didn't she want all of him, every part, every thought? But was this real? Could it be real? When he knew everything, would it still be real?

The touch of Rader's warm lips against her temple reminded her where she was. "Rader...just hold me." His strong arms held her close and she snuggled against him, holding on to what she could have of him for as long as she could have it.

"Everything will be fine, honey."

"Will it? Will it ever be all right? There's so much between us. I wanted you so much...."

His fingers stroked the side of her face tenderly. She turned and placed a kiss in his palm. Rader cupped her face and brought her lips up to meet his.

All the warmth was there, all the giving. But Rader knew Fancy wasn't fully awake or fully aware of what she was doing. When she came to him, he wanted her to know everything involved in a relationship with him. And he wanted to know everything about her.

"I want you in my life, Fancy Connors."

Fancy roused a little from the sleep pursuing her. "Our lives are very different."

"Let's not worry about that right now."

"I'm merely being realistic," she murmured. "I'm a very realistic woman."

He smiled down into her face, his thumb tracing her closed eyes. "Are you, now? I could think of other words, like insufferable, untenable, shrewish, stubborn...." Then his voice dropped an octave and his fingers began to caress her chin. "Beguiling, bewitching, enchanting."

"I thought you didn't like me."

"That was my problem. I liked you too much. I couldn't get you out of my system."

"But you were so solemn, so determined. I didn't think you'd even remember me...."

"Ah, Fancy, you're a hard one to forget. I've always been a man who took things very seriously. That's one of the things I had to learn to temper. Taking yourself too seriously only leads to trouble. Unfortunately, I didn't learn that soon enough to help you."

"Rader..." She saw his throat move as he swallowed.

"Now, before this gets out of hand—" he brushed the backs of his fingers against her cheek tenderly "—I've got to get up."

Rader slid away from her and stood. She watched him slowly button his shirt and shove it down into his jeans. He seemed amused by her open perusal of his body, and warmth suffused her when he grinned. "Do you approve?"

"You have a beautiful body."

"And you, my sweet lady, are perfection itself."

Rader wrapped the blankets around her again before cradling Fancy in his arms. Dropping a light kiss on the tip of her nose, he smiled down at her. "Before this gets out of hand, you're going back upstairs."

The next morning, Fancy awoke slowly. She lay thinking about what had happened the night before, halfway between sleep and wakefulness, worrying the words and nuances.

"How do you feel this morning?"

Rader stood in the doorway dressed only in lowriding jeans. He'd obviously just come from the shower and was still toweling his hair dry.

"I'm fine."

He read the wary look on her face. "Are you?"

Her gaze swept over him and his body reacted obviously. "Don't look at me like that," he warned. Her wide, golden eyes were slumberous, though a teasing glint lit them.

"Why not?"

"Because when you do, I want you and it's not the right time. When we finally make love, I want it right. Perfect. A hundred things have to be settled first."

Cold apprehension mixed with warm anticipation inside her. "Such as?"

"Nosy. Brian's coming. I promised to look over some contracts before he arrives."

"I suppose Brian is your principal advisor?"

"Pretty much. Though I do have an investment counsellor for certain things."

"I guess he's your closest friend."

"Brian and I are more than friends. We're almost like brothers. I'd like you to be my closest friend."

Frown lines appeared on her smooth forehead. "I don't understand."

"You will. Would you like a shower?"

She recognized his evasion. "Yes. But I can handle it myself."

He smiled wryly. "You've been handling things yourself for too long. Let me help you."

Her gaze fought with his. "Now, get into the shower," he insisted gently. "You have five minutes before I bring breakfast. I know Miriam is fixing something special to tempt you. She's been very worried about you. So has Paul."

A shadow came into Fancy's pale face. "Rader? What about Sharon?"

Rader sat on the side of the bed. "Honey, Sharon has nothing to do with us. I know you thought there was something between Sharon and me, and I have to admit I encouraged that idea a little to make you jealous. But there was nothing there. Never has been."

"But those nights you were away, I thought you were with her. Paul said you weren't, but I didn't believe him."

"Believe it. I stayed away because I couldn't be in the same house with you. We were always tearing at one another and I couldn't stand that any more. I had a lot of things to think through, so I drove a lot, walked. I should have been working, but I couldn't think straight with everything between us."

She wanted to believe him, but she was afraid to.

"Then there was Paul and your relationship with him."

"Paul and I are just friends."

"I know that now. We talked a long time after I brought you in."

"And?"

"And—" Rader stood "—I know he wanted more, but you didn't. That's something we'll have to talk about." He tucked an errant strand of silken hair behind her ear. "I wish I could just take you away somewhere to soak in the sun, turn brown and healthy again, and make love to you until we're both old and gray. But for my own peace of mind, as well as yours, we need to get a few things straightened out between us."

His hand cupped her face tenderly. She wanted so badly to believe that everything had changed between them, like some miracle, but she couldn't. There were just too many secrets. Too many lies.

Fancy recovered quickly during the next two days, spending most of them downstairs on the couch. She was on her way back to her room in the afternoon when the doorbell rang. When she answered it, Brian Carter stood there with briefcase in hand.

"Fancy! How nice to see you up and around. When I spoke to Rader a few days ago, he was very worried about you."

"Thanks, Brian. Come in. Rader's waiting for you in the study, I think."

Brian came inside but stopped Fancy when she started upstairs. "I've got some things in the car for you. I'll bring them in after I've spoken to Rader."

Probably more fashion magazines, she thought. Mona subscribed to everything. "Fine. I'll see you later."

Fancy picked at the food on her plate through dinner, half listening as Brian and Rader discussed business. Finally Rader laid aside his napkin.

"If you're finished pushing that food around, Fancy, I'd like you to join Brian and me in the study. There are several things we need to discuss."

Her apprehension heightened. "You've been very mysterious the past couple of days. What's this all about?"

"You'll see," he said, standing.

Fancy followed Rader down the hall with Brian following. All kinds of questions and doubts flooded over her as she entered the room that held so many memories. She sat stiffly on the couch while Rader paced the floor. Brian, always the professional, seated himself in a chair adjacent to Fancy in order to face them both.

"First of all, Fancy, you know, I'm sure, that in connection with his role as executor of Mona's estate, Rader asked me to look into a few things for him."

"About me and Mona?"

"Yes. And I did so, with some reluctance. I felt some of the requests were...outside his role. But now, I'm glad I followed through. Some of what I've learned will make some differences in the disposition of Mona's estate.''

Fancy shot Rader a sharp glance. His face was strained and he looked uncomfortable. ''When I initially asked Brian to check into some things, I only wanted proof that you were like Mona. What he found has put a much different light on things. But don't judge me too quickly. I was so hung up on Mona, I wasn't thinking very straight.''

''I don't understand.''

Rader's hands were thrust deeply into his jeans pockets as if he couldn't trust them to be free. He carefully kept a distance between them when he faced her. Fancy didn't like what she was sensing and her stomach tightened with apprehension.

''Brian, would you begin?''

Chapter Thirteen

Brian cleared his throat as if he, too, was reluctant to delve into whatever he'd brought with him.

"Fancy, your mother's death was unexpected and untimely, for a number of reasons, one of which was your own hospitalization. I learned you'd been in the hospital for about five days when the plane crash that killed Mona and her...companion...occurred. I wasn't aware at the time that you had checked yourself out of the hospital because of the crash.

"When I was finally able to talk to your doctor, he told me he refused to sign the release papers because he wanted you to spend at least a month recouperating, then another month with restricted activity. You were warned, specifically, against returning to the routine you'd maintained prior to your hospitalization."

Fancy chewed her upper lip nervously.

"Rader, I don't think we need to go into this. What good can it do?"

"Just listen, Fancy. It's important to me."

"Why? Why is all this so important? It—"

"Because I feel like . . . Look, if I'd known the real situation, I could have made things a lot easier for you."

"I feel guilty as hell myself," Brian said. "There was no reason for you to pack all of Mona's things for storage. It wasn't even necessary for you to attend the funeral. In fact, you'd have been better off just going to bed for another two weeks."

"I needed to do those things. It made it all...final," Fancy explained.

Brian shrugged, his distress at his own insensitivity quite evident. "I never thought of it like that."

"I talked to Alfonso and to some of the students at the school. They miss you."

"I miss them, too. I'll be glad to see them again." She sent Rader a questioning glance. What was their future after today?

"How did you meet Alfonso and begin teaching?"

Fancy picked at a callous on her finger. "By luck, really. I've always loved music. In high school, there was a non-credit class in basic guitar. I took it and was hooked." A small smile curved her mouth. "I bought a secondhand guitar without Mona knowing it and practiced whenever she was gone. The teacher gave me extra lessons on his own. Mona would have had a fit. She hated musicians. She was always talking about how worthless my father was."

Rader's face was hard when Fancy glanced at him. "Go on."

"Well, I quickly out-distanced the teacher. By then, I knew I wanted to play classical guitar, though I still kept my old flat top. Then, he read about Alfonso starting a school and taking only a few promising students. I auditioned."

"And you were accepted."

Her strange eyes gleamed in the firelight. "Yes. And it was worth everything."

"Even the teaching after hours?" Rader asked.

"Yes."

"And singing at The Blue Note weekends?"

"Yes." She held his gaze levelly, determined not to compromise what she'd done. Rader had to love her for herself.

Brian cleared his throat. "From what Alfonso said, your days were quite often ten to twelve hours long, especially when you spent individual time with some of the students. I heard from several disappointed parents that their children would be spending more time in the classroom since you aren't teaching there anymore. It was quite a tribute, believe me."

"Thank you. I loved teaching."

"Then I talked to Rolando. He says to tell you the group he has in there now will go the instant you come back. How did you get that job?"

Fancy was tired of the inquisition. "If you talked to him, then you already know."

"I'd like to hear it from you," he said gently.

She sent Rader a quick glance. He had a taut, waiting look and a muscle jumped in his jaw.

"I needed the extra money. I talked to some students, some musicians, and the position was mentioned. Not many people choose the classical or Spanish guitar. It's difficult, the music's different, so, for entertainment purposes it's perfect. When I spoke to Rolando, he wasn't providing any musical entertainment for the dinner hour but was considering it. I talked him into trying me for a couple of weeks, just to see how it went. The gamble paid off." She flicked a look at Rader, who was listening intently. "I loved performing."

"From what I've learned and from your doctor's opinion, it wouldn't be wise for you to consider it for a while." At her look, Brian continued. "Look, Fancy, you were on the edge of a breakdown. Exhausted. Anemic. Developing a beauty of an ulcer. It was a blessing, the doctor said, that you had that appendicitis attack. If he could have, he'd have put off the surgery until you were in better shape. What made you do it? Why did you drive yourself so hard?"

She swallowed. "You must know the answer to that by now."

He relaxed back in his chair, his gaze holding hers. "I think I do, but I'd like to hear your version."

In desperation, she appealed to the dark, silent man across the room. Once he knew it all, he'd know too much about her. She'd be too vulnerable.

"Rader, I don't want to do this. I don't want to talk about this tonight, or ever."

He knelt in front of her as Brian paced to the other end of the room. "Fancy, I have to know it all. I've carried around certain ideas that were completely unfair to you. I condemned you without knowing all the facts. It was unforgivable of me. But you've done something even worse to yourself. You sacrificed your life, your talent, almost destroyed your health, for an empty shell of a woman you loved because she happened to be your mother, in the physical sense of the word only. She was never a 'mother' for you."

Fancy had paled noticeably but Rader continued. "The only way I know how to deal with something this important is to bring it all out into the open. Brian needs the information so he can complete his legal responsibilities toward you and Mona, and you need to know how we've both been victims of her selfishness."

"I don't want to do this."

"Please. For me. For yourself."

"Why? So you can keep me from getting my inheritance?" She grasped at straws. She didn't want to talk about Mona. "That's what this is all about, isn't it?"

Rader's face darkened and he ignored her question. "Tell me the truth, Fancy. What drove you to a collapse!"

She dropped her gaze and stared at her hands. Brian returned, carrying a steaming mug of coffee that he handed to her. "Shall we go on?"

Fancy sought refuge in anger. "Why don't you just tell the whole sordid little story yourself!"

Brian ignored her outburst and sat down. "Okay. First, Fancy, I've spent the last several weeks looking into Mona's business practices, checking bank deposits, safe-deposit boxes, stock certificates, bonds, anything I could get my hands on. A certain pattern began to emerge. Lest I come to any wrong conclusions, I'd like you to clear up a few details for me.''

"Such as?" She refused to look at either man.

"What was the principal source of Mona's income, in your opinion?"

Fancy felt dizzy. Her hands shook so badly she had to set the coffee aside. "Her money came from investments. I suppose from Kurt's estate."

"Tell me about Mona and Kurt...and about you."

"There's nothing—"

"I want to know the truth, Fancy," Rader interjected. "I've been so wrong about so many things, I want to know the truth."

Fancy finally looked up at him. She studied his face for several moments, knowing that she was saying goodbye. Once Rader knew everything, all his promises would be forgotten. There would be nothing left for them.

Finally Fancy began to talk quietly, her hands clasped together so tightly, the knuckles were white. She dredged everything up from deep inside, and it hurt like a scraper against tender flesh.

"Mona was exactly what you thought she was, Rader. She was shallow and vain. Everything you accused her of being.

"You know how beautiful she was. She could look so innocent. Ask so prettily for things. There were a lot of men, but Kurt was the only one I remember with any...fondness."

She took a deep breath and continued. "He used to call me on the phone...just me...when he was out of town. We'd talk for a long time. Then he'd bring me something. A gift. Something silly like bubble gum or a comic book. He was...a very loving, caring man. I missed him terribly. When Mona started seeing... seeing men...when Kurt was away, I was furious with her. I can remember yelling at her, and she just laughed. She was so certain her beauty could buy her anything...."

Fancy's voice trailed off, but Rader prodded her again. "Come on, honey. Talk to me."

Her amber-eyed gaze searched his face. He met it, trying to make her understand that he knew how difficult this was for her, that he would share her pain if he could.

"It was always you, Rader. Only you."

His fingers fondled a soft strand of hair that had fallen across her shoulder. "I know, honey."

"You were so special to me. You were the big brother I never had, and yet, you didn't fit into that category, either."

Fancy stood and began to pace the room, looking everywhere but at the man who listened so intently. "Then you were gone. The arguments between Kurt and Mona continued. It was during those arguments that Mona began throwing her exploits up to Kurt. It was during a particularly furious argument that Kurt suffered his attack. It was awful. I went to the hospital and stayed with him, holding his hand, talking to him." She stopped at the French doors and looked out into the darkness. "And then he was gone."

When she didn't continue, Brian prodded her.

"What happened then?"

"We left here. Mona already had someone in mind when Kurt died. He was married, with two children. Wealthy. You see, the care and feeding of Mona Connors meant a lot of money. Keeping up the image, a little tuck here or there. And then one must maintain ones contacts by being seen in the right places with the right people, in the right clothes. It all cost a lot of money and Mona was not one to stint on herself."

"Where did you fit into all of this?" Rader asked softly.

"I didn't fit in. I didn't want to. I made my own money. Paid my own way."

"From the time you were fifteen?" This was from Brian.

"Yes."

"And then what happened?" Rader asked.

"Something awful." Fancy paced the floor again. "Mona became ill. At first she ignored the symptoms, but I guess she finally became concerned enough to consult a doctor. I came home one day and she was in a terrible state. I'd never seen her like that. She was crying and pacing the floor."

Fancy paused, then continued. "For the first time in my life, I saw her afraid of something. Thinking about the future. Her makeup was gone, her hair tumbling down, and she was dressed in a robe, pacing and shouting like a mad woman. When I finally got her calmed down, she told me the doctor had confirmed she had a serious illness. There was surgery, treatment, therapy, but she couldn't face all that, she said. What she couldn't face was the prospect of being less than perfect. That was what she saw, you know. The prospect of being ugly."

Fancy paced, her arms crossed in front of her, her hands rubbing her upper arms as if she were cold. And she was cold. Inside, where nothing could reach to warm her.

"I finally convinced her to at least consider surgery. I talked to her doctor, then convinced Mona to go to the hospital. But it cost money. A lot of money. I didn't have any.

"So I took on more hours at school, kept the job at Rolando's and took the job at The Blue Note. Mona had the surgery. I'd never seen her so afraid. It was like she believed that if her beauty was marred in even the most superficial way, it would be her complete destruction. Nothing I could say would convince her otherwise."

Fancy stopped and stared out into the darkness again, almost forgetting the two men listening so intently. "I could never understand her fixation with her beauty. Maybe she didn't understand it, either."

Turning back to the room, she continued. "Well, Mona had the surgery and things went well. Fortunately for her ego, she found someone. A man who could support her emotionally as well as give her some financial security for a time. But somehow, her relationships were never lasting." Fancy bit her lower lip contemplatively. "Mona had difficulty making real commitments. She could never care for anyone more than herself."

Realizing she had strayed from the subject, Fancy began to pace again. "Anyway, I kept working, juggling the money to pay the bills, and Mona continued therapy."

She turned to Brian then. "I guess the rest is obvious. Mona met Carl Hendrix—never letting him know about her illness, of course—and they went to Texas. On the way back, the plane crashed. I don't know for certain when they left because I was in the hospital. And now you know it all."

"Yes," Rader affirmed. "It's all over."

Fancy studied Rader at length. "Yes. It is, isn't it." Then she quietly left the room, gently closing the door behind her.

Brian and Rader spent over an hour in the study with the door closed before Rader found Fancy in the kitchen and asked her to rejoin them.

"I thought everything had been said."

"It's our turn," Rader said. "Mona's estate has been probated and all the details are completed."

"Is there anything?" There was still the matter of Fancy's own unpaid bills.

"Very little," Brian said. "There's Mona's jewelry, which comes to you, the apartment furnishings and personal effects. I'm afraid it isn't much, in light of everything you've done to maintain the life-style Mona expected and to pay for her medical expenses during treatment. It doesn't begin to repay you nor give you much to start a new life."

"It's all right, Brian. I didn't expect much. I just hoped."

"What will you do now?"

"Go home. Start over again. But this time, I'll do it for myself."

Brian leaned forward and caught her nervously-twisting hands between his.

"I wish I could have done more." He opened his briefcase and took out a small box. "While I was digging into Mona's affairs, I learned a great deal about you. There aren't many people as strong or as forgiving. You understood Mona's pain and fear and her selfishness. You tried to stand between her and the harsh realities of her illness, and for a while, she was able to live the fantasy that everything would remain the same. You gave her a special gift. Even if she didn't tell you, I think she must have known how precious a gift it was."

Tears spilled over and Fancy let them flow. "Thank you."

"There are a few pieces of jewelry left over." Brian handed her the box.

Fancy lifted the lid and smiled up at Brian. "Kurt gave her these."

"Yes. I think he'd like for you to have them."

She closed the box and held it to her chest. "Thank you. I always loved these."

"I'll walk upstairs with you now," Rader said. "It's late and you need to sleep."

Fancy went with him, knowing she probably wouldn't be able to sleep. They stopped at her old bedroom and her heart sank. "Brian and I still have some things to talk about and you need some time to think. But if you want anything, just call. I'll always be here."

She nodded numbly and went inside, closing the door softly. Rader was right. She needed to be alone.

* * *

Brian and Rader were finishing breakfast when Fancy came downstairs the next morning. She could tell from the papers scattered over the table that the men had been there for some time. Rader poured her a cup of coffee and one for himself.

"Did you sleep all right?"

"Fine," she lied, sipping the coffee.

"These are for your records," Brian said, shoving some papers toward her.

Fancy picked them up and stared at them uncomprehendingly. There was a copy of her hospital bill and beneath it an invoice from the physicians group to which her doctor belonged. Across each statement was stamped the word PAID.

"I don't understand." She seemed to be saying that a lot lately.

"Well, when Mona's story began to unfold, and yours, I learned how you were being pressured for payment by these people. I talked to Rader and we agreed that I should sell some jewelry from Mona's estate to cover these expenses. We both felt that, under the circumstances, it was the thing to do." He smiled understandingly. "We felt you would refuse a loan or gift from Rader."

Fancy swallowed, struggling to hold on to her composure. "I—I don't know what to say. I didn't know what I was going to do about these bills."

Rader ran a hand across her shoulders affectionately, giving her a gentle hug of reassurance. "I wish you had come to me about this."

"I couldn't, knowing how you felt about Mona . . . and me. We weren't your responsibility. Besides, I couldn't give you any more ammunition against me."

As if they were the only two people in the world, Rader smoothed her hair over her shoulders. "I'm sorry I made things so difficult for you."

"Ahem, before you two forget I'm here, there are a couple more things we'd better take care of."

Fancy blushed, and Rader laughed aloud. "He's right. Brian has a surprise for you."

"Something else?"

"Come into the study."

Fancy followed the two conspirators, seeing the significant glance between them. At the study door, they stood aside. She looked from one to the other in question before seeing the surprise they'd promised.

"Oh, Rader."

Her own guitar rested in the seat of a chair, gleaming and inviting. She ran forward and cradled the instrument lovingly in her arms.

"Paul told me you'd left this in storage. After I saw how much music meant to you, I asked Brian to find it."

"Thank you. Thank you, Brian. You don't know how much I've missed it."

He grinned. "I can hardly wait to hear you play." He picked up his briefcase. "I've got a flight and I'm cutting my time thin. If there's anything I can do for you, Fancy, just let me know. Rader, just send those contracts to me with a cover letter whenever you're ready. But, I wouldn't delay too long.''

Fancy and Rader watched Brian's rental car until it was out of sight, then returned to the house arm in arm. Inside, Rader turned to Fancy.

''Well, where do we go from here?''

''I don't know.'' Her chest grew tight and she was afraid to think.

''Well, let's start with the real reason you accepted my invitation to come here.''

Remembered pain prompted her hesitation. ''I told you.''

''I want the truth.''

''Why did you invite me?''

''We're very good at games, aren't we? I guess we've both had a lot of practice at that.''

''Yes.''

His lips curved in a smile. ''I asked you because I remembered a coltish girl who brought innocence and sunshine into my life. I wanted to see if there was any laughter left.''

''Even though you believed I was like Mona?''

He shrugged. ''What I believed and what I wanted to believe were always at war. I wanted us to spend this summer together to make peace.'' His gaze locked with hers. ''Why did you come?''

When she finally spoke her voice was barely audible. ''Because I wanted peace, too.''

''What was the name of your war?''

"The same as yours, I guess. I love you, Rader. I've always loved you."

He released a long breath. "I've waited a lifetime to hear that."

Relief flooded through her. "I've waited a lifetime to say it."

*   *   *   *   *

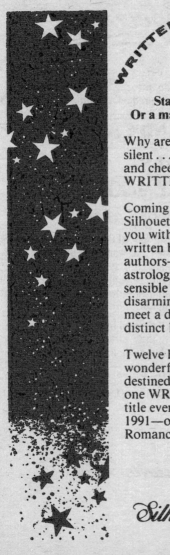

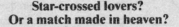
WRITTEN IN THE STARS

**Star-crossed lovers?
Or a match made in heaven?**

Why are some heroes strong and silent . . . and others charming and cheerful? The answer is WRITTEN IN THE STARS!

Coming each month in 1991, Silhouette Romance presents you with a special love story written by one of your favorite authors—highlighting the hero's astrological sign! From January's sensible Capricorn to December's disarming Sagittarius, you'll meet a dozen dazzling and distinct heroes.

Twelve heavenly heroes . . . twelve wonderful Silhouette Romances destined to delight you. Look for one WRITTEN IN THE STARS title every month throughout 1991—only from Silhouette Romance.

STAR

Silhouette Books®

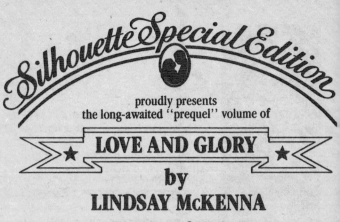

Silhouette Special Edition

proudly presents
the long-awaited "prequel" volume of

★ LOVE AND GLORY ★

by
LINDSAY McKENNA

Dawn of Valor

In the summer of '89, Silhouette Special Edition premiered three
novels celebrating America's men and women in uniform: LOVE
AND GLORY, by bestselling author Lindsay McKenna. Featured
were the proud Trayherns, a military family as bold and patriotic
as the American flag—three siblings valiantly battling the threat
of dishonor, determined to triumph . . . in love and glory.

Now, discover the roots of the Trayhern brand of courage, as
parents Chase and Rachel relive their earliest heartstopping
experiences of survival and indomitable love, in

Dawn of Valor, Silhouette Special Edition #649.

This February, experience the thrill of LOVE AND GLORY—from
the very beginning!

DV-1

❧ Silhouette Books

Take 4 bestselling love stories FREE

Plus get a FREE surprise gift!

Special Limited-time Offer

Mail to   **Silhouette Reader Service®**

In the U.S.
3010 Walden Avenue
P.O. Box 1867
Buffalo, N.Y. 14269-1867

In Canada
P.O. Box 609
Fort Erie, Ontario
L2A 5X3

YES! Please send me 4 free Silhouette Romance® novels and my free surprise gift. Then send me 6 brand-new novels every month, which I will receive months before they appear in bookstores. Bill me at the low price of $2.25* each. There are no shipping, handling or other hidden costs. I understand that accepting the books and gift places me under no obligation ever to buy any books. I can always return a shipment and cancel at any time. Even if I never buy another book from Silhouette, the 4 free books and the surprise gift are mine to keep forever.

*Offer slightly different in Canada—$2.25 per book plus 69¢ per shipment for delivery.

Sales tax applicable in N.Y. Canadian residents add applicable federal and provincial sales tax.

215 BPA HAYY (US)   315 BPA 8176 (CAN)

Name   (PLEASE PRINT)

Address   Apt. No.

City   State/Prov.   Zip/Postal Code

This offer is limited to one order per household and not valid to present Silhouette Romance® subscribers. Terms and prices are subject to change.

SROM-BPADR   © 1990 Harlequin Enterprises Limited

SILHOUETTE·INTIMATE·MOMENTS®

NORA ROBERTS
Night Shadow

People all over the city of Urbana were asking, Who was that masked man?

Assistant district attorney Deborah O'Roarke was the first to learn his secret identity . . . and her life would never be the same.

The stories of the lives and loves of the O'Roarke sisters began in January 1991 with NIGHT SHIFT, Silhouette Intimate Moments #365. And if you want to know more about Deborah and the man behind the mask, look for NIGHT SHADOW, Silhouette Intimate Moments #373, available in March at your favorite retail outlet.

NITE-1

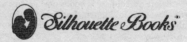 Silhouette Books™

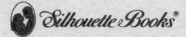

Silhouette romances are now available in stores at these convenient times each month.

Silhouette Desire
Silhouette Romance

These two series will be in stores on the 4th of every month.

Silhouette Intimate Moments
Silhouette Special Edition

New titles for these series will be in stores on the 16th of every month.

We hope this new schedule is convenient for you. With only two trips each month to your local bookseller, you will always be sure not to miss any of your favorite authors!

Happy reading!

Please note there may be slight variations in on-sale dates in your area due to differences in shipping and handling.